MANIFESTATION

ARPIT TANEJA

Contents

Contents

Contents

Acknowledgements

THANK YOU

TO MY FAMILY AND ALL THE READERS WHO ENTRUSTED ME AND MY WRITING...

AND INVESTED THEIR PRECIOUS TIME IN {A SMILE TO BRIGHTNESS} {UNFULFILLED DREAMS}

Prologue

This book is a work of fiction, and I do not want to hurt any religious sentiments.I respect every religion. *Please read it as fiction.* Certain information I have included in this book is available on the internet. Do not indulge in any activity described in the book.

Note: - some parts are intentionally manipulated or spelled wrong for the safety of readers and myself...

1

At Talks

***

Welcome everyone to another enticing episode of AT Talks with Ayesha, your friend, adventurer, host, and fool for stories and knowledge. I never thought I would receive much appreciation and love when I started this podcast, but you all made this journey enjoyable.

But today, I feel more eager than usual because this show's lovely and precious audience has requested this guest the most. As you all know, we aim to spread knowledge and help our listeners as much as possible.

I have seen this name after every show in the comment section for the last three months, especially regarding psychology-related topics. Every time I saw that name, I looked at the calendar and the date, but not anymore. The day is here when we will hear from one of our society's prominent personalities.

Please welcome Mr. Viren Arora, Ganganagar's youngest psychiatrist. Not only is he one of the girls' favorites for his charming looks, but he is also one of the most reputed personalities our city has seen, whether as a psychologist or for his caring nature towards the environment and his patients.

First, Mr. Viren, I would not lie; I have patiently waited for this day. It's an honor to have you on our show. And I can't wait to gain knowledge from you and apply it to my life to be a better person than yesterday.

Viren: Thank you for having me on the show. I apologize to you and your lovely audience for making you wait so long.

Ayesha: Sorry for my reaction, but I am amazed by your looks and voice. They are so soothing and manly at the same time. I certainly can look at you all day, but your voice is one serious distraction.

Viren: I didn't expect to blush this early in the podcast.

Ayesha: Haha, but before we dive into some serious topics and the questions that I have prepared for you, I have a question that's purely out of curiosity and came to my mind as soon as I saw you. If you don't mind, can I?

Viren: Curiousness is a beautiful art of our mind. So go on.

Ayesha: - After a long, tiring process and research, we learned you have been on a break for a year. We saw your picture on the hospital walls and Google, but you look different today. You have long hair and a thick beard instead of tiny hairs and a clean shave [which I am not complaining about; you are looking way more dashing and irresistible]

Viren: - It's a long story.

Ayesha: Well, one undeniable thing in our country is a "story." Undying love for stories is a quality and virtue of our society.

Viren: But if I start narrating this story, we will not have enough time for the questions you prepared.

Ayesha: It's not an issue. Now that we have a hold on you, we can make this a two-part or special podcast. I promise your audience won't complain.

Viren: [after a long sigh of relief] I think I need closure too. Okay, let's do it, but before that, you need to answer two of my questions.

Ayesha: - Perfect! This episode had started on unexpected terms. I love it...

Viren: - you must have heard about Dhruv Sharma [Hanumangarh News, 2022].

Ayesha: - yes, it still gives me shivers.

Viren: - I met him in 2022.

Ayesha: - (perplexed) Okay.

Viren: - one of the most challenging scenarios I have faced in life was his. But before I go into the minute-by-minute details, my other question is,

"Do you believe in Supernatural power/ paranormal activities?"

2

2022

GANGANAGAR, 2021

Kanak pg., Jawahar Nagar

Piyush: - Dhruv, Dhruv...

Yeah, I heard you.

coming...

Piyush: What are you doing, Dhruv? We will miss the lecture. It's already 8:45, and for your information, our lecture starts at 9:00

[Upon reaching downstairs]

Why are you shouting like a man possessed with mad dog powers? College is just 2 km from here, and I am more excited to see her than you are about the lecture.

Piyush: Dhruv, you need to understand that it's our final year before we dive into a phase of job-finding and helping our family. It would be best to focus on studying rather than her; she has been with us since the first day of college, and from what I remember, she rejected your proposal multiple times.

[With irk written over my face]

Yeah, I know, I still won't accept defeat. One day, she will accept me.

[Piyush shakes his head in disappointment]

Piyush: - You are helpless, and why in the world does it take so much time to get your ass out of that unhygienic pg—room of yours. Don't tell me you, of all people, decided to clean it yourself.

The room is pretty clean, and it's your mindset that needs some broom cleaning *[agitated]*

We both got off the bike and saw our classmates moving toward the class, so we asked them to wait for us.

But soon, my legs declined to move as I saw her entering the premises. Piyush looked back and knew.

Piyush: - Let us move guys.

Classmates: - What happened to Dhruv?

Piyush: - Nothing, "Nidhi is back from vacation."

Everyone looked at her and started giggling

But they don't [see what I do.

"Nidhi" *[is a perfect mixture of beauty and poise; she carries herself with grace written all over her personality, her deep brown eyes can put a river to shame, and her long black untied hair makes me wonder what is slickest. Her skin or her hair? His smooth skin expresses her rich genes, his lips naturally curved, showcasing the smile and her voice so musical that it puts me in hypnotic sleep]* **was wearing a black crop top with blue denim jeans.**

As she passed by my side, my eyelids decided to reserve my looking sense so I could smell the perfect blend of strong and light cologne she wore. The only words that chose to come out were

Hayee...

I started moving so that I could align my foot with her footprint. It's been six years since I first saw her on the first day at Bihani College, and at that very moment, I said, "I am in love."

Piyush: - Hi Nidhi,

[This asshole, "Piyush," we have been best friends from what time it was. I don't even remember; we were four or five years old. We have been together through thick and thin; it was in 2013 when Piyush's mother left us, and I remember my mother [Manju Sharma] raised Piyush as her older son... I have been pampered more by my father [Kamal sharma]. We have seen brawls, heartbreaks, and love together. But whenever he talks with Nidhi, I feel like killing him. Not only him, if I ever see somebody try to bring discomfort to Nidhi, I feel a rage to kill that person]

Even though Piyush is my best buddy, it still boils my head when I see him talking to Nidhi.

Piyush: - Dhruv, Move fast, man

Upon hearing Piyush, Nidhi stopped, looked back, and said; hi, Dhruv, sorry, I didn't notice you.

A sense of calmness entered my body upon hearing my name from her.

Hi, Nidhi. It is not an issue. I was looking for a box in the bag, so you might not have noticed me [I lied]

Before she could say something, Piyush's over-enthusiastic brain questioned, "Box?"

I wanted to hurl abuse at his ass but decided against it as Nidhi was looking at me.

I made a fruit cake

Piyush: - Cake? With questionable eyes

At this moment, I wanted to beat him to a pulp, but to his rescue, Nidhi extended her hand towards me and asked for the box.

Nidhi: You made it for me and were not looking for the box. I know you were looking at me from the gate to this point. You won't change.

As I handed her the box, she smiled and said, "he is dumb."

Piyush asked me to move, but I got lost in her smile. Then he screamed, and my happiness was cut short.
"I won't give up"

3

Manifesting Her To Be Mine

Why do these professors have to behave so efficiently near the exams? Or why do I have to attend these lectures continuously? Can't I have a break of about 24 hours after every lecture?

Piyush: - Because not everybody is as careless as you, and now don't make a face; your thoughts are visible on your face.

Sometimes, I cannot understand how he knows what I am thinking. Is he some psychic?

But why am I still sitting in this lecture? I should move out, but whenever I try to leave the class, she makes me stay {not by saying but as soon as I look at her,} I decide to stay.

So, let me focus on her rather than this lecture; Piyush will help me during the exam. I know for sure this man can be a pain in the ass, but he has never left my side, whether it's a situation at home, a brawl, or a study.

Piyush: - Stop looking at me. I am not Nidhi.

How the hell does he know? He is psychic.

But leave him; I should focus on my happiness; there she is, listening to every word of the professor. Her face during class shows not only innocence but also sincerity. Her eyebrows and frown forehead, whenever she cannot understand a topic, make me wonder why she doesn't hear me this seriously.

Wait, what? Does it make any sense, but that's how madly I love her.

She caught me staring at her, which is normal. Even after getting the indication that she would see me, I was not able to look away, which irked her. Her angry eyes asked me to look away and focus on the lecture.

I still remember when she caught me staring at her for the first time. She scolded me after the lecture, and I was standing with my head down, not in shame, but Seeing her this close made my heart swell with happiness, and I was afraid that rather than hearing her, I would be daydreaming of kissing her.

This incident happened a few times, but when I proposed to her for the first time, she stopped scolding me. After that, it was either her angry eyes or her ignorance that made me believe I still had an existence around her.

Well, that doesn't change the fact that I did propose to her several times to hear a "NO," and only the first time she reacted loudly; it was apparent when I thought about it. It was just one week into college, and she had already caught me staring at her thrice. Rather than hear her scolding and understand her, I said I love you, and Damm, I must say she did control herself from slapping me.

After that, she said no and moved away blatantly whenever I proposed. But still, if I wanted to converse with her, she never said no.

But I am not going to stop. This is our last year in college, and I will propose to her in a week. I have entirely manifested the day and daydreamed about it a hundred times.

MANIFESTATION

"Manifesting her to be mine."

4

I will accept my fate

***

Piyush: - Dhruv! Have you lost your mind? *[well, it was as loud as an opera singer, but him being an opera singer doesn't give a good imagination]*

Man, my ears can't take your shrilling voice. Pitch down a little.

Piyush: Do you want me to calm down? You know what? You have lost your mind to the extent that you cannot see that she is uninterested.

But one day, she will accept me. *[why am I sounding like a loser?]*

Piyush: Okay, I am calm now, but look at you. "You are one good-looking boy, with a 5ft 8 inches height, a fully grown beard, and long smooth hair enhancing your looks, not to mention your non-conventional eye color and well-maintained toned body, famous among girls from the school time for your looks." And you are running behind a girl like an obsessed man, troubling her.

I know I have troubled her and you enough, but she will accept me now. I have entirely planned this. Please believe me.

Piyush: - what if she says no again? *[furious]*

She will not.

Piyush: - what if? Dhruv, what if.

After complete silence for a few minutes, **I said I will accept my fate.**

Piyush: - you promise that. Does a brother promise?

Yes, I promise, accepting his handshake to make it a deal.

Piyush: Then, I believe, and I wish I would call her Bhabhi, not Nidhi, after that day.

So, what's the plan he said as he hugged me.

"I promise I will accept my fate."

5

I want to make it grand.

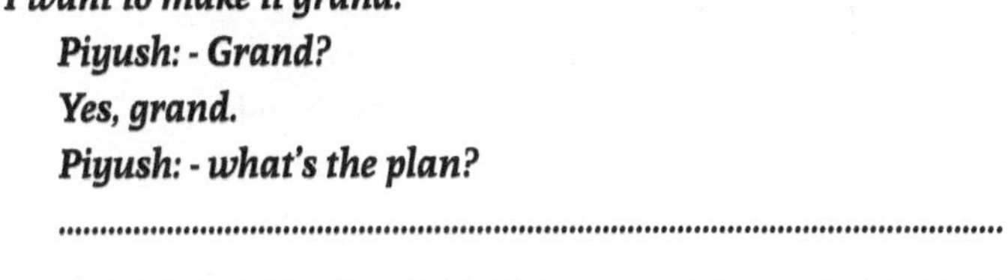

I want to make it grand.

Piyush: - Grand?

Yes, grand.

Piyush: - what's the plan?

....

....

She deserves everything that I am about to do. No! She deserves way more.

Piyush: - I don't want to be a party spoiler, but Dhruv, I don't think you should do this.

Piyush...

Piyush: Now, don't make a puppy face. I will help you. But it would be best if you would not forget about your promise.

NEXT DAY

I knew Nidhi would never be late for college, so I finished the preparation early...

Piyush, please do not mess up the timing. Where is everyone?

Piyush: - stop behaving like a cat. Everyone is at their place. {I am still unsure if Dhruv should do this because she will say no to him. Even though I was not sure what I would

have said when he told me about his plan, I should have stopped him}

{what's the plan, Dhruv?

Let's go, I need to buy something for her.

Piyush: - What exactly do you want to buy at this hour of the night

"jhumke"

Piyush: - jhumke?

That's why I say you will never be able to see her the way I see her. Whenever anybody talks about her jhumke, you should have watched her eyes: "Those glistering eyelashes, her kid-like smile." She can talk about her jhumke for a whole day.

Piyush: - You want me to look at her?

Not only will I wipe that smirk off your face, but I will kill you if you ever repeat things like this...

Piyush: Woo, woo, calm down. I was kidding. Hey, come on, let me help you choose.

Just shut up, I know her more than you ever could; show me that silver color, not that, the long rounded one, yes, yes, that one.

Piyush: - I am impressed... now what, Dhruv?

Inform everyone not to react animatedly tomorrow.

We will meet tomorrow, so don't forget to do what I said.}

Piyush: - I have put jhumke and the letter on her table as you said...

{Nidhi, I know you would be angry after seeing the letter but I promise you this will be the last time that you will be bothered by me. I will be waiting for you at the same place where we met for the first time- at the volleyball ground}

"can't wait to see her."

.

.

.

Piyush
I knew she would react the same way she is right now. She is furious. Not only did she tear the letter, but she crushed his gift.

[I was getting bad vibes from the time when Dhruv decided to make this proposal materialistic rather than expressing it with pure emotions and understanding. But I wanted this to end once and for all. Nidhi might not say it, but she is fed up with Dhruv's antics [brawling with others for Nidhi, staring at her in class, and following her everywhere.]

[To make things worse, the whole class started hooting when Nidhi picked up the letter and gift from the table. It infuriated her, and she yelled at everybody and broke the Jhumka.]

I should have stopped Dhruv, but it's good that both Dhruv and Nidhi will be free from this torture after today.

"Sorry, Dhruv, I knew she would say no to you all along."

6
Miserable

I can't wait to see her. I hope she likes my gift; no, I'm sure she would have loved it.

Everything seems beautiful today: fresh air, tree leaves, chirpy birds, and even the whole college seems different. I am sitting in the middle of the college on the volleyball ground, looking toward the class, waiting to get a glimpse of Nidhi. I can already imagine the joy in her eyes when she looks at the gift. She would be looking for me after seeing the gift, but Nidhi, you deserve more... I can't wait to show you the picture I edited for you. I can't wait to show you the short stories I have written for you.

I am smiling like a kid at the mere thought of the moments I will share with you, sitting together, talking, and smiling at each other.

Here she is,

looking as gracious as always in the black Punjabi suit...

Hi, Nidhi

Before I could say anything, she slapped me. She didn't even let me say anything and forgot about executing the plan. I prepared to make this day unforgettable...

I asked my other friends to be ready with the photos I had given them earlier and told them to stand behind me when I formally proposed to her, but I didn't expect the turn of events that unfolded. She slapped me...

Nidhi: Enough, Dhruv. I am ashamed of you and myself. I was wrong; I should have slapped you on the first day for your nonsense. You made my college life a living hell, and I am warning you now: don't even look at me from now on.

And bamm {this slap is for you to remember how much I hate you}

She slapped me again}

Piyush: - {I knew things would get bad but didn't expect the following events. The Whole class followed Nidhi to see what would happen, and well, it turned out worse than I thought} {Dhruv was careless, and to be honest, he brought all this on himself} {the news spread like a fire in a forest, the whole college was buzzing with the events. Dhruv became a hot topic in college, but for all the wrong reasons}

Piyush: - Dhruv, open the door, man; what are you? A teenage girl, Dhruv...

Creak...

Piyush: - Dhruv

I remember my promise.

Piyush: - are you drunk?

It's a happy day, brother. Now, I will not trouble you and her.

Piyush: look at you; you cannot even walk properly. Come, let me take you to your bed. How much do you drink?

Ouch, wait here. Something gave me a sting in the leg; let me turn on the lights

what the fuck, six bottles of beer? Are you out of your mind, Dhruv... sit here.

[I haven't seen Dhruv this drunk... he was not able to stand on his feet for more than thirty seconds, and the room was full of ash and smoke can't even count the cigarette butts on the floor he was blabbering in intoxication] [i tried my best to make sure he doesn't fall, but now he is laughing lying on the ground. I should make lemonade, but I don't think it will work] [I went into the kitchen, and I found cigarette butts there also; he had utterly lost it, and thank god I found a lemon in his kitchen]

Piyush, you knew she would say no; you are a psychic man.

Piyush: - shut up and drink this.

Umm umm, leave me, what is it?

Piyush: - lemonade... drink it. *[I have to use my force to make him drink lemonade; if he were not that drunk, he would have overpowered me]*

I thought everything would be fine... but...

You were correct; I tortured her, and I made a fool of myself, thinking she would accept me one day. I am sorry, Piyush, I made your life miserable too.

"I made her college life miserable."

7

His eyes

Piyush

Everyone is laughing at Dhruv. It's been a week since the incident, but neither Dhruv nor the college has stopped talking and thinking about that day.

The girls who used to look for a chance to talk to Dhruv were laughing at him now. The juniors who used to fear him are making fun of him. The boys who got beaten by him for Nidhi are intentionally teasing him.

But what I am fearing is Dhruv's behavior; he has been drinking every day, passing out due to intoxication, smoking weed, laughing for no reason alone, and blabbering, "She slapped me." I know he would never harm her, but call it my intuition or fear, things look bad.

On the other hand, Nidhi is still furious. Whenever she enters the class, I can see her anger for Dhruv. Dhruv immediately leaves the classroom as soon as she enters. It feels like he only waits until he gets her glimpse before leaving.

"My brother neither forgets about that day nor can he move on from her."

I hope he won't do anything wrong to himself or "her."

Dhruv, Dhruv... [It has been 15 minutes since I have been knocking at his door, and now my anger is turning into fear; open the fucking door, Dhruv]

Piyush: Don't tell me you have started drinking in the day now. Open the door.

Come in and have some beer,

Piyush: - Are you serious? We have to go to college and look at the room; beer bottles are everywhere, and cigarette butts seem to be in the hundreds. Do you want to commit suicide? Please let me know; I have less painful ideas for you... even better, I can kill you with my bare hands. [I can't tell the relief I got looking at him. This boy is a brat, but he is not the wrong person. He is careless but protective. He goes heads down in a brawl for his people without caring about his health]

Monster... haha haha...

You forgot the date, it's her birthday, I can't attend college.

Piyush: - What the hell with this now? I dread the day when you entered my life. [I think my intuition was wrong; even after getting slapped by her, He is trying his best not to ruin her birthday]

Like her... haha

Piyush: - [I never thought I would see a day when I will see him crying, he can hide everything, but his tears are failing him] **Damm, okay, give me a beer... fuck you.**

Marry me, Piyush...

Piyush: - Get your hand off me.

Piyush, I never wished harm on her... I truly loved her... but she didn't even think for a second before slapping me... not once but twice...

Piyush: - [what's going in his head? I have never seen him angry while talking about her; I should change the topic] **Let us watch something; where is the remote? Here it is...**

What are you looking for? It's been 20 minutes, and you are just changing channels. Stop, stop. This podcast seems interesting...

Piyush: - umm, bull shit, tantric on the podcast; everybody wants to be famous nowadays... and if I am not wrong, this is a local podcast.

Yes, let's see what he is saying...

{tantric: - two things I want to convey, which is on arisen in youth, black magic to kill somebody and "karnapisachani"}

Piyush: - What bull shit is he saying, natural entity... and black magic.

Black magic to kill somebody is interesting.

Piyush: - what the hell are you blabbering? Let me shut this off...

.

.

.

Piyush, let's go...

Piyush: - huh! Where? [what does he want now? Please don't say tea; I can't take that bullshit routine of his. Who the hell drinks tea after alcohol]

College... get up...

Piyush: - no, sit down... we are...

Shh, I want to see her...

Piyush: - [I wanted to say no, but looking at his eyes, I got afraid] Okay, but don't create a scene outside of college.

I want to look at her...

"Black magic can kill somebody?"

8
Words

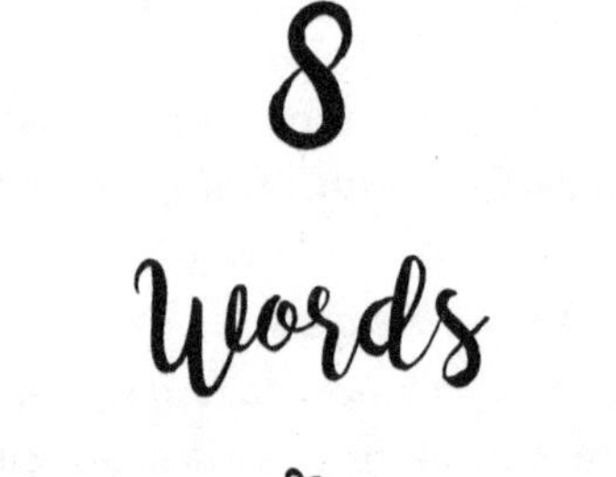

Piyush: - Dhruv, stop smoking. A professor might see you...

[I am afraid we are going to get caught because of Dhruv; he is smoking profusely, and there are many known faces I don't want to see right now. Everyone is looking at Dhruv. I stopped the vehicle as far as I could, but people around the college knew us because of all the brawls Dhruv got in. He has punched many people because of me and Nidhi... his anger is no secret for the college. He even got into brawls with outsiders for Nidhi, and I see many faces here because of Nidhi's birthday. Everyone is giving a stare to Dhruv, but this guy gives no fuck to them. He knows he is strong, but I believe he is a badass rather than strong.]

Who cares?

Piyush: - Dhruv, stop...

[suddenly, a known face caught my attention, and this was the last person I wanted to see here with Dhruv being Drunk]

Dhruv, isn't he Mayank, the one whom you beat to unconsciousness last year when he threatened Nidhi?

[last year, an outsider was creating trouble for Nidhi; he followed her for a week, and fortunately for him, Dhruv was in Hanumangarh then. He asked Nidhi for a date many times.

Still, she used to ignore him, but one day, he threatened Nidhi and said he would make her life miserable if she didn't accept his proposal. But his luck ran out when Dhruv returned, and seeing Nidhi tensed, he created chaos in class to know what happened; he shut the class door from the inside and didn't let teachers enter the class until Nidhi narrated the whole incident. He got a warning from college for his antics, but they didn't know bigger chaos was about to break down.]

[Dhruv left the class ten minutes before, and as a good friend, I had to accompany him; honestly, I wanted to make amends with him because he was angry at me for not letting him know the situation in college and not protecting Nidhi. I said I have seen him. I will help him recognize that guy. but I didn't account for what happened when Dhruv and Mayank came face to face]

[I thought Mayank would be a proper match to Dhruv's Strength, looking at his physique, but it was one of the most one-sided brawls of Dhruv I have been part of or looked at... Dhruv didn't even let Mayank land a punch. Mayank face took the beating of a lifetime; he was bleeding from his eyebrows, and his nose, a cut near his lips was visible, and his shirt was torn into tatters. The professors tried their best to stop him, but they got punched, too; Dhruv was uncontrollable till Nidhi decided to interface.]

[but I have to accept that was one beautiful scene I witnessed, the guy who was uncontrollable by four professors was controlled by a girl's hand; Nidhi moved forward and put a hand on Dhruv's chest, and Dhruv stopped to call it a push by Nidhi would be an insult she just placed her hand and Dhruv started moving backward looking at Mayank screaming in pain on the ground. Everyone was shocked. Some girls were in awe of Dhruv's manly behavior, and some were in awe of the scene. Dhruv was moving backward, and it seemed Nidhi was pushing Dhruv back.]

[he was suspended for a month, but we never saw Mayank near Nidhi again]

Huh! I don't remember, and why would I? Do you remember every mosquito you squashed?

Piyush: - it seems like the badass Dhruv is returning, Dhruv, here she comes...

Huh! As usual, she is looking beautiful.

[I was getting bad vibes seeing Mayank, and vibes didn't lie]

Piyush: - Dhruv, Mayank is approaching her... you are drunk, so please be calm. *[I was trying to erode a rock by air]*

I am calm and here to get a glimpse of her. I am not going to create a scene.

Piyush: Let us move from here. I know you won't be able to control seeing somebody talking to her. *[Have you ever seen a person slamming his head to the wall?]*

Shh!

Piyush: - Dhruv!

[okay, Mayank made a howler. I don't know How Nidhi felt when Mayank grabbed her hand, but I skipped a beat. The visuals of the Dhruv-Mayank brawl and its effects are still fresh. Dhruv's father has to use his influence to keep Dhruv out of legal action.]

Nidhi: - How dare You, Mayank. Leave my hand.

He shouldn't have done that.

Piyush: - Dhruv... *[as soon as I saw Mayank, I knew this was going to get south]*

Dhruv... *[Mayank is deadpan, and I will get in trouble again, and "maa" will be angry at me because of Dhruv. And to add to it, we are drunk]*

Dhruv... I knew you would create a scene.

Nidhi: - leave my hand, Mayank.

"boom" [okay, a few faces started to disappear. Dhruv's Strength is insane.]

Do not touch her.

Nidhi: - Dhruv, Piyush?

Mayank: - You of all people, I think you forgot she slapped you...

Who cares, but did you forget I was the one who beat you to unconsciousness...

Nidhi: - Piyush, stop him... and what is this foul smell? Are you both drunk?

Piyush: - umm, I should stop Dhruv. [I was feeling embarrassed]

Boom [voice of another punch startled us] [oh shit, "Rukja Bhai" Dhruv, stop]

Piyush: - umm, Dhruv, stop...

Don't even think of moving from there, Piyush... [his voice emitted a warning vibe]

Piyush: - what has gotten into him?

Listen, Mayank, let me tell you something... please forget her! And if I see you again near her, "I will kill you."

And look into my eyes; I am not joking...

[Dhruv's tone was calm but cold-blooded]

Nidhi: - Piyush! Stop him... his tone suggests he is serious...

Go away, Mayank... Go Away... I yelled

Piyush: - [I wanted to move to help and stop Dhruv, but his words sent shivers to me, "I will kill you" had a freezing effect on me... before I could move, I saw Mayank leaving and Dhruv approaching us with the same intensity in his eyes] I am sorry, Nidhi... we did not mean any discomfort to you.

Let's go, Piyush...

Piyush: - [is he changing, or is he too drunk? He is ignoring Nidhi]

Nidhi: - Dhruv, I don't need your help... and I told you to...

Shh!

Piyush: - {am I dreaming... Dhruv Just did that; he said "shh" to Nidhi}

Don't think so much of yourself... I did nothing for you; honestly, I want you to hear me carefully...

Piyush: What the hell did I hear? He got close to her, which scared Nidhi, and said, "Love or hate......................."

{Love or hate, happiness, sorrow, blessing or pain, only I have the right to inflict it on you. Nobody else can take this away from me, nor will I allow anybody to take it from me... I will protect you from others so you can enjoy the fear I see in your eyes because of me.}

Piyush: - I need to protect her to keep Dhruv safe.

9

What's going on in your mind

Piyush

It's been a week since Nidhi's birthday, and Dhruv has completely changed... he is acting weird {weird would be an understatement}.

He is not leaving class like before and drinking as usual, but nowadays, he disappears from his room. Yesterday, I saw him, hearing that tantric, "Is he thinking of..." No, it can't be true; my mind is playing tricks.

Even Nidhi seems different. I caught her looking at Dhruv many times, but she was not afraid of him; she appeared tensed for Dhruv.

"But what's going on in your mind, Dhruv?"

....

Dhruv

{tantric: - two things I want to convey, which is on arisen in youth, black magic to kill somebody and "karnapisachani"}

.

Karnapisachani!

Google isn't helping. I should dig deep and go to the dark web, "karnapisachani."

[Karnapisachani is a Sadhana with the help of which negative entities around us are controlled and made to work. There are positive and negative entities (spirits) roaming around us. Since managing the positive energies can be difficult, maintaining the negative energies can still be accessible. However, it is easy for only those who know how to complete the Sadhana without letting the hurdles disturb the entire process. A Sadhak must know how to complete the Sadhana.

The entities that are used to get the work done through the Karnapisachani process are lusty, have high sexual powers, and can do anything to have their sexual thirst fulfilled.]

Sexual desires! This information is not enough. I want to know more about it.

But how could I? The web is not enough. But how?

How?

How?

Tantric, yes, I should meet a tantric.

[tantric: - two things I want to convey, which is on arisen in youth, black magic to kill somebody and "karnapisachani"]

Yes, I should meet that tantric. He can help me. I should look for his number...

Google: - param podcast, episode 18, 98812...01

"She slapped me," "karnapisachani," "Sexual desires," "black magic can kill somebody?"

.

-next morning-

Piyush: - Dhruv, Dhruv...

I have something important to do. I will not accompany you to college...

Piyush: - don't die. *[should I stay with him? He is acting weird.]*

Huh! Get lost...

Tring Tring...

Hello, thank you for calling the param podcast helpline. How can we help you today?

Hi, I want to meet Tantric Shikhar. Can I get any contact info or address?

Sure, I will provide you with his assistant number... 97722...11

Tring... Tring...

Hello...

Hello, sir. I got your number from the Param podcast; I want to meet Tantric Shikhar Ji...

I will send you the address... beep beep

Huh! That was quick.

You received a text message.

....

Hi, Piyush. A familiar voice brought me out of my thoughts, "Nidhi."

[Thank God Dhruv is not here. I don't know how he would have reacted to this.]

Hi, Nidhi...

Nidhi: - Sorry to disturb you, but you seemed stressed... everything fine?

[Should I share everything I am feeling regarding Dhruv's situation? But why is she concerned about me?]

Yes, I was thinking about Dhruv... I am sorry about that day.

Nidhi: - it's okay. I wanted to talk about Dhruv...

[oh, scrap that first thought. She is not concerned about me. But did she say Dhruv? Fuck... Did Dhruv do something to her?]

Dhruv? Did he do something? *[my reaction was the proof of my thoughts]*

Nidhi: - No, It's just that...

You seemed tensed,

[for the first time, I saw her low on confidence. She was evading eye contact]

Nidhi: I wanted to thank him for that day, but my ego didn't let me, and I realized I was harsh towards him even the day I slapped him. Don't get me wrong; I am still unapologetic about slaps, but what I said to him was uncalled for. He protected me from everyone and every time. He was there whenever I was in trouble.

He can be a little painful, but he always cares for his people and considers you his responsibility, his close one... I replied

Nidhi: - But what I saw in his eyes on my birthday was shocking, and when he said, "I will kill you, Mayank." At first, I thought that was a heat-of-the-moment expression, but when I saw his eyes, it was cold but fearsome "he was not kidding."

His behavior is weird, and I am sorry about it.

Nidhi: I am worried about him, and it scares me when I see you alone and not him. Is he fine?

He says he is fine, but his behavior tells a different story.

Nidhi: - he is drinking too much, right?

Yes, he is, but it's not the only worrying sign... his anger, passion for you [which I term obsession], and subtle changes in his day-to-day activities are more worrying signs.

Nidhi: - Can I help him?

I don't know; I hope he will be fine one day...

10
Let it be

Dhruv

2:00 PM

What's this place? A tattered house outside the city? {what is it, a movie?} I might be at the wrong place, but the location shows I am in the right place.

It's outside the city, and I have traveled 12 km to be here. I hope this is not the wrong destination.

I should ask somebody...

there is a tea vendor... I should ask him

{excuse me, is this house of tantric Shikhar}

He looked at me as if I committed a crime.

{tum yaha Kya krne aye Ho? Why are you here? Yes, this is the house. These kids nowadays don't understand and take these things as an adventure. Go away rather than going into that house.}

What an odd man.

Knock... knock...

I am Dhruv... I called you in more......

Tantric assistant: - come in.

Huh! He didn't even let me complete what I had to say. And the stairs to the basement? Without any natural light...

these artificial lights are merely a formality. I should look after myself, or else I will fall.

{I will lie to myself if I call this a place. Walls were about to fall, it seems; it was neither a small place nor a large house. The whole place was stinking, and as soon as I entered the place, I felt like puking.}

What the fuck is this foul smile {somebody killed the mouse here or what?} Oh, finally, some light... here he is acting efficiently to impress me, "Tantric Shikhar," reciting some hymns offering fruits to fire, but what is that idol behind him that is smaller than what we see in movies but comes to think of it I haven't seen a goddess like that enlarged idealistic body, thick thighs, curvy body, colossal boo... umm, shut up Dhruv she might be a goddess. You are committing a sin, and what made you sexualize an idol, you have lost it.

Tantric: - what do you want?

Information...

Tantric: - information? About what?

Karnapisachani.

Why are his assistants looking at me like I have asked for their life?

Tantric: - and who do you think you are? And why would I give you more information than I told people on that podcast?

Because I want it and don't think of myself as a fool, you went on the podcast for this reason only: "You want people to approach you; you want to get recognized."

Tantric: - still, why would I tell you? Is it because a dumb person like you got fascinated hearing about "karnapisachani"

I want the information...

Tantric: - {smirking} I see hate in your eyes... anger to harm somebody... but still, why would I tell you?

Whatever I have read till now, I have been fascinated, and I want to know more.

Tantric: - you can leave.

I am ready to pay whatever amount you ask for...

Tantric: - why would I tell you? Leave now...

I want to know what powers I will acquire after "karnapisachani sadhana."

Tantric: - so, I was right. You want to harm somebody or maybe many... but you are too timid for that. I will tell you something: you are too naïve to think there are no consequences, and "karnapisachani sadhana" is easy.

I might not want to harm somebody, but I want to know more...

Tantric: Okay, sit down. You said the powers, "She will give you everything you need till you fulfill her desire," but if you let her control you, "YOU ARE AS GOOD AS DEAD."

Desires?

Tantric: - sexual desire, alcohol, chicken, and "loyalty," you still didn't get it?

Baba Ji, I want to know more...

Tantric: - if you have "karnapisachani" in your life, you won't be able to get close to any other girl... even to your mother, sister... "IF YOU DO, IT WOULD BE FATAL"

I skipped a heartbeat hearing this...

Tantric: She demands sacrifice and has her desires. She is not a paranormal entity; she is a supernatural power.

I will leave...

as I was leaving, I heard tantric laughs. It sent chills to my bones.

.

.

.

.

Piyush: - Dhruv, where were you? I was worried... I need to tell you something...

Huh! I went to meet... nothing, you say

Piyush: - Nidhi asked about you today... Dhruv, Dhruv... {Why is he zoning out?}

Huh! It doesn't matter anymore...

Piyush: - Dhruv! {he seems lost, and why does he smell different and by the looks of it, he is smoking profousely}

Shh... I need a cigarette. Do you want one?

Piyush: - {he is genuinely different, and it's fearsome, and why do I feel he was somewhere where he should not be} Okay, you alright, Dhruv?

Yes...

I should not think about what happened today, and this will not occur...

It seems more of a fiction, but still, it's dangerous...

"Let it be"

Piyush: - {I hope he is not getting into something that changes the course of our life}

"I hope"

11

Would be fatal

—♡—

It's been two days, but still, I can't get over his words: "Even to your mother, sister... "IF YOU DO, IT WOULD BE FATAL."

.

.

.

Nidhi
{Love or hate, happiness, sorrow, blessing or pain, only I have the right to inflict it on you. Nobody else can take this away from me, nor will I allow anybody to take it from me... I will protect you from others so you can enjoy the fear I see in your eyes because of me.}
Why do I think about him? Did I make a big mistake? Did my action harm him? Were my words to him even justified?
I should talk to him...

.

.

.

Piyush
What is he thinking? Even during the lecture, he seems utterly lost. He didn't even notice Nidhi entering the class. He is not leaving his room nowadays. He got into a brawl with

juniors who taunted him. It seems he is losing himself...

.

.

.

Dhruv
"She will give you everything."
Nidhi: - Dhruv,
What does she want now? But I should not forget she was respectful towards me before that day when she slapped me... and hate to accept her smell makes me weak... "Yes," I replied
Nidhi: - I am sorry for that day...
Distinct chatters: - for the slap you mean {haha... haha...}
You did it intentionally.
Nidhi: - No Dhruv
I got it. You want to embarrass me. {she intends to keep that day alive in everyone's memories, she wants me to suffer.}
Piyush: - No, she is genuinely sorry...
Shut up {I smashed my hand onto the table to let everyone know if they don't stop laughing, I will make you pay}
Nidhi: - Dhruv, I didn't mean it
You did, but I like this fear in your eyes... I will be the one who will inflict that fear, only me...

"karnapisachani"

12

I hope

Piyush: - You were wrong today. And stop smoking; it's your 3rd stick on trot...

Stop behaving like a mother. Didn't you see she intentionally brought that incident in front of everybody? {why does everyone think girls are always right? Why did she bring that topic up today? And if she was sorry, she would have texted me or talked privately.}

Piyush: - No, she just apologized.

I am going somewhere and will meet you tomorrow.

Piyush: - Going where?

None of your business...

Piyush: - {Before I could say something, he accelerated his bike and left}

I have no time to think about what will happen; I want power and everyone to be afraid of me.

Knock... knock...

Assistant: - What are you doing here at this time?

Tantric: - Bring him in... I knew he would return.

I folded my hands. "Namaste"

Tantric: - Your anger and hate have brought you here again, but why would I help you?

I want power. I want to make people suffer... I know after hearing this you might not help but... {before I could complete my sentence, he started laughing.}

Tantric: - Who said I won't help? But will you be able to complete the procedure? And even if you. Your desire won't let you live...

Sorry?

Tantric: - If you succumb to her desire and let her control, then you will be a "SLAVE, not a MASTER," and that is also subjective: "WHETHER YOU WILL BE ABLE TO COMPLETE THE PROCEDURE?"

What's the procedure?

Tantric: - 1 lakh cash.

1 lakh!

Tantric: - Nothing comes free in this world...

But 1 lakh...

Tantric: - I am pretty sure your desire for power is more precious than 1 lakh.

Umm, okay...

{It's been an hour since I left the tantric's place. I have been looking at the bank balance, and it's pretty substantial. I know Piyush thinks I am careless, but in the last five years, I have refrained from making any unnecessary demands or expenses, which my father is proud of, so he never refuses. Should I ask for money from my father? I should, I want power at any cost}

Papa, I want some money...

Papa: - how much?

20,000/- {why am I getting anxious?}

Papa: - This much money, why?

I want to get my bike modified...

Papa: - You bought that bike last month; I will transfer the money, but is it necessary?

Yes... *[I had been smoking for an hour, and hearing this, I threw away the cigarette and was getting all excited]*

Papa: - okay, I will transfer it.

I knew my father would not deny it; as I said, I haven't made an unnecessary request in the last five years. I even saved money by buying an old bike, which my father is unaware of... 78000/—in my bank account + 20000. I need 2000/—more... I can't borrow it from Piyush... I need to do something...

What should I do? Where is the envelope? My parents gave it to me on my birthday, so it's time.

-next morning-

Knock... knock...

Tantric: - Seems so desperate...

What's the procedure?

Tantric: - Before that, you need to know something more...

{consider this as a warning: it is not safe... I thought you would leave hearing the price, but you are persistent. If you make any mistake during the procedure, she will kill you... if you are not able to tame her, you will be doomed not only till death but for the next 1000 years...}

What is the procedure?

Tantric: - {smirking} you are blinded by your anger... okay, I warned you, but it's your choice.

{The procedure will continue for three days, but before giving you the mantra, you need to understand something...

For three days, you have to feed on your excreta. You have to drink your urine and eat your dung. There is nothing else that you can do to survive.

__karnapisachani__ is going to appear nude in front of you, but you cannot touch her. She is allowed to do sexual things to your body, but you cannot. You have to resist it. If you give in, your Sadhana breaks.

Your entire life, you have to have sex with __karnapisachani__. There is no other woman you can ever have sex with. If you are planning to get married, it is not possible. If you are married already, __karnapisachani__ can kill your partner.

Even if you are lethargic and not in the mood to have sex, you still have to satisfy __karnapisachani.__ There is no escape from it. Remember – no matter how easy and pleasing this sounds, it becomes frustrating.

Some people have committed suicide due to denying having sex with __karnapisachani__ after a specific time.

Once __karnapisachani__ is invoked and impressed, she whispers the future into your ears. Even if you sleep while thinking of a specific question, she will whisper it into your ears when you are sleeping. You do hear her loud and clear. Even the slightest mistake can ruin your entire Sadhana and life.}

I am ready...

Tantric: It requires a perfect setup, but don't worry; my assistants will handle that. Again, I will say, "DON'T DO IT," or if you still are willing to, "DON'T LET HER MAKE YOU HER SLAVE."

I will be waiting for your call...

.

.

.

"Assistant: Guru Ji, does he want to die, or what?"
Tantric: - I pray nothing happens with him.
We all thought it was just a myth when we started it, but what happened last year made me a believer...

Assistant: - But knowing that, should we not deny him?

Tantric: - Would you deny 1 lakh? We started this as a business, and don't forget there were many cases before last year which prove last year was just an unfortunate incident for that man, and he committed suicide... so no one will ever be able to prove us crooks. Haha... haha...

"I just hope he doesn't die here... haha... haha..."

13
But what if

———♡———

It's been a week; I haven't received Tantric's call. Should I visit his place or wait for a while?

[I was in deep thought regarding what happened in this past month. I understand what went wrong, but she overlooked everything I did in five years for her, and it was not about the slap. It was those words that hurt me]

Tring... Tring... [phone buzzing brought me back]

Hello...

Assistant: - We will start the procedure today.

I was waiting,

Piyush: - For what?

Huh! You startled me... nothing. I have to go to a relative's house. I will be back in three to four days...

Piyush: - relative?

Yes...

Nidhi: - Dhruv,

Huh! What's with you both? First Piyush, and now you. I felt scared. Stop calling my name out of nowhere.

Nidhi: - Can I join you both?

No...

Piyush: - Have a seat, Nidhi, and you dare to get up from here, Dhruv.

Nidhi: I know, Dhruv, you are hurt and angry, but I am still unapologetic for what happened except for my words...

I don't feel like listening to you...

Piyush: - Behave yourself...

Nidhi: - shh, Piyush... I said what I had to say,

"Don't make a mistake, Dhruv, that will haunt you forever."

.

.

Assistant: - he is coming...

Tantric: - I hope you know what you have to do and don't repeat the mistake of leaving his body unclad when you go to dump him.

Assistant: - Guru ji, you are so sure he will die.

Tantric: - He will die of lever infection; you know what he will be consuming...

Assistant: - But what if?

"Shh, he will die..."

14

Don't let her tame you

---♡---

***It's time Dhruv** [should I do this?]*

Knock... knock...

Assistant: - Come in.

***What the fuck... what's this foul smell? It's more than usual.** [leave sadhana; it seems this tantric wants to kill me. I would faint from the smell]*

Assistant: - shh!

***Namaste!** [Did he overdress, or did he consume some weed? What the hell is this costume? He is wearing a necklace of bones. Well, he seems to be a movie lover.]*

Tantric: - Sit down...

What's going on here? Is this a corpse? Why are there bones? I can understand the foul smell, but...

Tantric: - Remove your clothes.

***Huh! Okay.** [what is with these guys? They never let me complete the sentence]*

Tantric: - You remember what I said?

***Yes...** [I should focus now.]*

Tantric: - Give him the chit.

[Om Aim Hreem Shareem Dum Hum Phat Kanak Vajra Vaidurya Mukta................. Ahe Aakash Mam Karne

Parichay............ Bhoot Bhavishya Vartmaan Kaal Gyan Door Drishti Door Shravan am Broohi Agni Sabnam Sahtu Stambnam Shatru Mukh Stambnam Shatru Gati Stambnam Shatru Mati Stambnam Paresh am Gatim Maim Sarva Shatrunaam Vaag Aarambh Stammbaum Kuru Shatru Karya Hani Kari Mam Karya Sidhi Kari Shatrunaam Udyog Vindhya's Kari Veer Chamundani Hatakdharini Nagri Puri Pattansthan Sammohini Asadhya Sadhana Om Shareem Hreem Aing Om Devi Han Hum Phat Swaha]

"<u>The mantra has been edited to protect everyone. It's not meant to make fun... or disrespect any religion...</u>"

recite it for three days... and remember, "DON'T LET HER TAME YOU." We will leave you alone now... "don't make a mistake."

umm,

Tantric: - You still have a chance, but after you begin, there is no coming back...

I am ready...

.

.

.

I smell bad, and my stomach is aching... I will not stop. Om.................., why am I feeling dizzy? How much time has passed?

.

.

.

Munch, munch, munch... how much time has passed? It is still yucky, but I have nothing else to eat.

.

.

.

Munch, munch, munch...

15

I fucked up

Gulp, gulp... this alcohol doesn't seem reasonable too. I should not stop...

Why do I feel that I am in hell... my dung, urine, and puking all around the room. I cannot understand if my smell or rotten mouse smell is killing me, but I can't stop...

.

Tap... tap... tap...

Huh! Is it Guru Ji?

Guru ji... guru ji... guru ji... [why isn't he responding?]

Tap... tap... tap... [The voice of Someone approaching started to fill the room, and everything started feeling colder. Is it my mind playing tricks, or am I able to invoke her?]

.

.

.

Why am I feeling dizzy? Umm, Someone is approaching me. It seems like a woman figure. Who is she? Is she, "Karnapisachani"?

Is she Karnapisachani? or is my tired mind making up his dreamy land?

But no matter what, I should resist her...

But look at her...

What fair skin, wine glass curves, lusty lips... smooth long hairs... her glistering eyes... shh, shh, Dhruv, you must restrain yourself. [Tap... Tap... Tap...]

Umm, she looks way more gorgeous up close.

Shh... Dhruv, Do not let her control you. Keep on chanting those mantras...

Umm, she is touching me... umm, meditate...

Umm, stop licking me...

No, Dhruv, don't let her sit on you... keep on meditating...

Oh fuck... her bosoms are huge... don't let her... umm...

Dhruv... Dhruv... [Nidhi's voice broke my concentration. Why is she here? Is everything okay with her?]

What the fuck? It's Nidhi's voice, It can't be true.

Dhruv...

Umm, it's my mind playing tricks...

Dhruv, look at me...

She is not ni... umm, stop her from kissing you... recite the Mantra...

Dhruv! Let go of yourself.

Umm, umm, Nidhi... take me away. [seeing Nidhi this close, I want to let her take over me]

I need to hug her, or else she will be disappointed. But how could she kiss me with this smell...

Shh, Dhruv...

Umm, ah, never thought this day would come in this dark, untidy place... umm, ah, never thought Nidhi will be so good in bed {well, place doesn't matter, it's the same feeling...}

She is consuming me... how could she let me get inside her... umm, ah... ah... I will faint; stop it... stop it...

Haha... haha...

{who is she? It's not Nidhi's voice… who are you… ah, ah, ah, stop it…… who are you? I yelled in desperation}

.

.

.

Don't come close to me… *{yelling becomes more of desperate cries}*

Shh… who am I? You are my slave… I am your mistress…

{the shrilling voice echoed in the atmosphere, felt like my soul was the one whose cries it was}

Haha… haha…

"Ah… ah… I fucked up."

16
Where are you

—♡—

Tantric

Guru ji, guru ji...

Tantric: - What happened?

Assistant: - I heard him screaming in pain... [His body was trembling]

Tantric: - His lever must be giving up.

Assistant: - Guru ji, the scream was similar to the last time...

Tantric: - What do you mean? [his facial expression changed]

Assistant: - I think he gave in and...

Tantric: - shh, don't say bull shit... is he still screaming?

Assistant: - no...

Tantric: - let us check on him...

Tap... tap... tap...

Tantric: - Light up the torch...

[what the fuck... this smell can kill anybody, put on the mask]

Assistant: - there he is... is he dead, Guru Ji?

Tantric: - shh, let's check.

Guru ji... yelled the assisatant after checking Dhruv's Pulse...

Tantric: - What happened, say it, and what's with your face?

Assistant: - He is alive.

Tantric: - So, that means he was successful in invoking {still shocked but confident enough that Dhruv will die soon} *but got tamed.*

Assistant: - What should we do now? What should we do?

Tantric: Stop overreacting. It will be like last time. He will die soon. Now, get up, do as I told you, and don't forget to dress him... [he yelled at his impatient assistant]

Assistant: - if he tells everything to somebody... what will we do?

Tantric: - he was the one who wanted to invoke her... so stop sweating on a non-existent issue.

.

.

.

Piyush
Where are you, Dhruv?
It's been four days already. Not picking up my calls or replying to my texts...

"Where are you, Dhruv?"

17
Please Let me know

Piyush

Should I call his father to learn about him? But what if his father doesn't know?

{I know Dhruv, You lied to me. You are not in hanumangarh or at any relative's place. I should have confronted you, but I thought you would get better from a layoff. Where are you? It has already been four days, and I have no clue. Where are you?

Nidhi: - Piyush!

Huh! Hi Nidhi... how are you? *{I was startled, and it shocked Nidhi}*

Nidhi: - Dhruv did something?

No... Why?

{Did Dhruv do something to trouble Nidhi? Why is she asking about Dhruv?}

Nidhi: - You seem tense, and Dhruv has been absent for four days...

{Those words broke my resilience. I didn't cry but was on the brink of it. Everything that transpired in the last month has taken a toll on me}

I think he is doing something wrong; he is not picking up my phone, nor is he in his room... he said he would return in

three days, but

Nidhi: - Return from?

He told me he was going to his relative house. But I know he is trying to hide something...

Nidhi: - What can it be? And did you ask his parents?

No, I asked one of my friends to check whether he was at home, but he was not there...

Nidhi: - Piyush! I am not feeling good about it...

Me too...

Tring... Tring... [We were in the middle of a conversation when the mobile display showed "Dhruv"]

It's Dhruv...

Nidhi: - pick up... [her hasty response proved she was tensed too]

Hello, "bsdk," where are you? And why did you not pick up my call... where are you?

Stop shouting and listen to me first... [a girl's voice comes up with a response]

Who are you? How did you get this phone?

I am calling from govt. Hospital, Ganganagar... you should quickly reach here...

Beep... beep...

[it felt like this is not the disconnected tone. It's my heartbeat that will give up any second after hearing hospital]

Hello, hello... [I was shivering at this point]

Shit... shit... shit.

Nidhi: - What happened?

I don't know, I need to go to the hospital... it was from govt. hospital...

Nidhi: - What? Is he fine? [Nidhi's voice alerted the whole class]

I don't know... I will tell you later... I need to go...

Nidhi: - Please let me know...

[god... please protect him]

What the hell did you do, Dhruv? What will I tell Uncle and Aunty if something happens to you? And why am I crying? Is he my brother? No, he is just a badass brat who doesn't care about anybody...

[I was on my way to the hospital, but every passing second felt like an hour; my restlessness was taking over my mind]

Move away... why does the hospital distance seem more prolonged than usual...

"What the hell did you do to yourself, Dhruv?"

18
Critical

—♡—

Hello, I received a call from the hospital half an hour ago. My name is Piyush, and it was my friend's mobile... his name is Dhruv. {why is she looking at me like this after hearing Dhruv's name?}

[I'm not too fond of the hospital atmosphere; many are crying, many are sitting in depression, the smell of glucose, and dry blood on the floor. For me, the most negative atmosphere is of a hospital]

Sir, sir... he is here... [Whom is she calling?]

As I look back, a chilling sensation passed my body... "Police, what did Dhruv get me into?"

Hello sir, my name is Piyush... [With little courage, I had left]

Inspector: - Come with me...

Sir! What happened to him? {at this point, I was trembling}

Inspector: - shh! Don't talk much... just come with me.

Okay [I couldn't even think of anything positive at this point.] We stood outside a ward... and he said to look through a window and asked me, "Do you know him?"

I am shaking, about to faint, thinking I am being called upon to identify his body...but what I saw was more terrifying than I thought...

I saw him covered with Drips and an oxygen mask to help him breathe. Unconsciously, his body showed drastic change; he indeed lost some kgs. I tried to ask the Doctor about his condition but was interrupted by the Police and before I could give them any satisfactory answer the Doctor didn't tell me anything.

Doctor: - He was consuming something that was not poison but harmful enough to damage his lever, and not to mention he was drunk. His condition is critical, and we need to do some more tests to find his accurate situation.

I was profoundly thinking after informing Dhruv's father when Nidhi called me.

Nidhi: - Piyush, is he okay? [she didn't even let me say Hi]

It is terrifying and precarious; I still don't know what happened to him or with him... he is still unconscious... Police are waiting for him to wake up.

Nidhi: - Police?

When I saw him... his face was pale yellow... lever was about to fail... it's still in serious condition... reports suggest he was drinking for nearly three days... eating something harmful [not a poison] ... his whole body is stinking... it seems he has lost considerable weight, which is alarming.

Stop it...stop it... stop it... [A manly voice echoed around the ward]

What the hell? It's Dhruv Voice... I will call you later...

[stop it... leave me alone... stop it... ah... ah... umm, stop it...]

"STOP IT..."

"I ran towards his room but was stopped by Police. "Only doctors allowed." He was screaming his lungs out, and other

patients relatives gathered around the Dhruv. The Doctor tried everything to calm him but was controlled by sedatives only. His cries were heart-wrenching. Even the Police officer felt heavy and asked me, "Bache ko Kya pareshani thi?"

I sunken on the bench after asking the Doctor about Dhruv's condition, but there was no reprieve for me; Nidhi called me again...

Nidhi: - How's Dhruv? *[What the hell? No hello again]*

His scream was intense. it feels like it is still audible... it's been an hour since he stopped screaming.

What has he done to himself?

Nidhi: - What is the Doctor saying?

....

....

Doctor, why was he screaming?

Doctor: We are still unable to understand. We gave him a sedative as soon as we admitted him, but right now, he wanted to move, but he was not able to.... We need to check; did we miss something? Where are his parents?

....

....

Nidhi: - Piyush! It is best if you shift him to some private hospital...

We can't do it... can only happen after police permission...

Nidhi: - and Dhruv's parents?

They are on the way; I don't know what to tell them...

Nidhi: - I am sorry, Piyush

No, it's not your fault. It's him. He needs to be accountable for his obsession...

Nidhi: - but he will be alright, right?

I can wish...

[before I could say any further, I saw Dhruv's parent entering the premises, "Maa" was crying already, and I could

feel the desperation in their walk and eyes to know how's Dhruv]

okay, his parents are here... I will call you later...

[an uncontrollable mother's emotion, a tensed father not only about his son but his wife, the whole family entering a hospital feeling desperate to know about his son is one unbearable sight to watch]

Nidhi: - take care of him...

.

.

Piyush, where is Dhruv? What happened to him? Where were you at that time? How is he now? I want to see him. What is the Doctor saying?

Calm down, Manju, let him speak quips Dhruv's father [Mr. Kamal]

Maa, he is in a serious condition right now... The Doctor has been examining him.

[As soon as I said it, tears turned into crying, and it felt like something broke inside me...]

Don't cry, Manju. He will be fine. You know your kid is a fighter. But Piyush, why is there an inspector with you? His father said

Uncle, he was found in a peculiar condition, and looking at him, the Doctor called them...

Dhruv's dad: - what peculiar condition?

Leave everything; I want to see Dhruv first,... his mother said out loud before I could say something...

Maa, I will take you to his room... this side...

Piyush, I am angry with you too. I believe in you more than him; His mom said... [more of a scolding, I would say]

Manju, you know your son, if he is alright till now, it is because of Piyush... [Dhruv's father trying to pacify Aunty and at the same time taking my side]

I know that's why I am angry with him... Piyush is my older son... I believe in him, not in Dhruv.

His mother's words while crying about his son's condition made me cry... I hate Dhruv for making his mother cry... he has a mother, and that's why he doesn't understand the value of a mother... his mother never let me feel that I lost my mother nine years ago... she took care of me like a mother... and many a time kept me ahead of Dhruv...

"I hate you, Dhruv"

Piyush, looking at you... I know you understand... Maa said

Piyush: - sorry, maa... he didn't tell me he was going somewhere;

I would have never let him go alone...

I know Piyush... I know... that's why you are my elder son...

[I was angry with myself now, not for Dhruv but for Maa. I should have been more careful]

Maa, this is his room... but we can't go inside...

Why?

Umm...

Dhruv's dad: - Piyush... [I felt the questionable eyes without even looking at Uncle]

His lever is in a critical situation. Before I could say more, I saw Maa moving backward. Maa, maa...

As soon as I conveyed this message, "Maa" fell and started sobbing profusely

Manju... get a grip of yourself... His father said

Dhruv's mom: - but how can we see him then?

Maa, we can look at him through this window... but I will say don't. He is not in good condition.

Weep... weep...

Maa, he will be fine...

Dhruv's dad: - Piyush, come here... why does your word lack conviction?

Uncle, a few hours ago... Dhruv screamed in pain, and the Doctor is unable to determine the reason for that pain...

Hmm! But how did he come into the situation where I had to see him in the hospital?

Uncle, he was tensed about something... [I didn't want to bring Nidhi into this situation, so I tried to divert the conversation] *We need to transfer him to a private hospital...*

I will talk to the Doctor and the Police too...

"Why do I feel this is more critical than it looks?"

19

It's his fault

Dhruv's dad: - Piyush, we can transfer him only after he is stable.

    {doctor, doctor} Nurse's voice echoed around the ward, which caught our attention

Dhruv's mom: - Piyush, what's going on?

I will check... calm down.

Mam, mam what happened...

    {he is gaining some consciousness... have some patience}

Nidhi: - how's he?

He is trying to get consciousness...

Nidhi: - thank God... and what about shifting him to another hospital?

Only after he is stable.

{what happened to Nidhi? She is tenser than anything... now what's happening in her head?}

Nidhi, can I ask you something?

Nidhi: - Yes...

You have changed a little in the last few days.It is not your fault.

Nidhi: - I don't believe that it's my fault.

But?

Nidhi: I realized he was not wholly wrong; he always protected me. I should have taken care of my words. I want to make things better...

Hmm... I hope Dhruv recovers quickly...

Nidhi: - please keep me informed...

"I want Dhruv to enjoy her friendship after all the efforts he made..."

20

Please Leave me

Nidhi

Why am I thinking about Dhruv?

He brought everything on himself. He should have maintained dignity towards me.

I know he is a good guy, but he must have understood our present and future, and it is not the right age to get tangled into a complex situation termed a "Relationship."

But still, I should have been careful with my words... but the intensity in his eyes on my birthday was so pure.

Why am I smiling?

....

Piyush

Aah... aah... stop it... get away from me, stop it...

... ...

Dhruv's Voice {more of a scream} filled the fear in the hospital surrounding... 2nd time in two days...

Dhruv's Mom: - Dhruv? It's Dhruv's Voice, Kamal, why is he screaming? Kamal...

Dhruv's parents ran towards the ward, and my fear {that his parents would learn about the screams came true. I wanted them to leave, but they resisted, and if not for the Kamal uncle, maa would have slapped me"}. I followed them, and what I saw was more disturbing than yesterday...

He was unclad for no reason. His body was uncontrollable, three warden {male} was unable to hold him, he was screaming {stop it} {stop it} ...

Manju, "Maa," succumbed to the sight and cried until unconsciousness took over. I assured my uncle that I would take care of Dhruv and please look after "Maa."

After a few minutes, Dhruv's screams died down. He was sweating, and after a few moments, the Doctor said, "Please take him somewhere else; we cannot understand his situation..."

But Doctor, why was he screaming? Is it because of his lever, or is there any severe internal injury?

There is no internal injury that we diagnosed after every possible test... his body seems stronger when he is screaming, and after that, it feels lifeless...

Tring... Tring... before I can say any further... "Nidhi's call interrupted our conversation..."

PLEASE TAKE HIM TO ANOTHER HOSPITAL. I AM PREPARING HIS PAPERS, ARRANGE THE AMBULANCE AS QUICKLY AS POSSIBLE... *the Doctor said as he walked past me, and Nidhi heard it over the call...*

Nidhi: - So, Dhruv is stable now... that's good news.

Umm, not really... actually {as I was about to tell her about his situation... his Voice circles my mind} "Leave me." Who was he referring to when he said, "Leave me."

Nidhi: - Piyush... Piyush?

Huh! Sorry, Nidhi. He needs better treatment resources, so we have to shift him to another hospital. Before she could ask anything more, I requested her to call me later, as I had to arrange the ambulance...

Nidhi: - Piyush, Piyush! {beep... beep...}

What's going on with Dhruv in the hospital? And now Piyush is acting differently... I hope Dhruv is fine...

.

.

I need to arrange an ambulance first, then I will talk to the uncle... but first I need a smoke... you one asshole "Dhruv" "Leave me."

21

You are mad

Puff... puff... what a hell of a day... thank God, I found a cigarette shop near the hospital. How ironic a cigarette shop at the gate of hospital premises... and a bench to sit on while smoking.

To whom he was referring, "Leave me."

What did he get himself into? Did somebody torture him, but there is no external injury? But how did he lose so much weight in just four days... why did he smell so bad?

Stop overthinking till he gets better and quickly arrange an ambulance.

"Bhaiya, ye ambulance Kiski Hai?" [whose ambulance is this?]

Okay, ambulance: done. Now I need to talk to the uncle.

Umm... "Maa!" I am in trouble. I might be stinking with a cigarette smell... I am in big, big trouble....

Kamal: - Piyush?

Huh! Uncle... I went to arrange the ambulance... I said it loud, hoping that hearing it, "Maa," would not slap me.

And it worked. "Maa" didn't move an inch after hearing it and stared at me from a distance, looking curiously to know more...

I explained the whole situation and asked my uncle, "Which hospital do you find suitable?" so I could convey it to the ambulance driver.

Medanta! I got a reply, and as I was about to approach the ambulance driver, Uncle whispered, "Your "Maa" doesn't like people smoking... and handed me chewing gum."

How is Uncle so calm after seeing Dhruv's condition? An iceman or what?

I looked back and saw Superman, Dhruv's Father, still smiling and handling this situation calmly and efficiently.

Seeing him, I smiled too... [I don't even remember when I last smiled like this] I took out my phone and texted my dad...

"I love you, Dad." I just realized every father is a superhero...

Before I could put my phone away, I received Nidhi's text...

It's 1 o'clock. The little I know about her, she sleeps early... [I remember Dhruv pacing around in the night, just itching to talk to her, but...]

[Dhruv, Dhruv... why are you moving left and right at this hour of night... acidity?

Dhruv: - Huh! Shut your stinky mind... I want to talk to Nidhi...

Then call her... oh you are looking for a network...

Dhruv: - That's why I said not to drink more than you can handle... you asshole, it's midnight, and she sleeps at 11 ... and I am not a fool to become a discomfort to that peaceful face of her while sleeping...

How cringe... Dhruv, you should stop drinking, man...

Huh! Sleep, Piyush, you are a child to understand my feelings for her...]

Beep... beep...
Huh, another text...
Nidhi: -?
Medanta it is. We are shifting him to Medanta. It's already late, and you must sleep; it is already two hours from your sleeping time... I replied...

I informed the driver about the destination and started moving toward the Doctor's office...
Beep... beep...
Huh! Nidhi again...
Nidhi: - How do you know my sleeping routine?
Okay, I fucked up... I should have been careful; now Nidhi will be angry hearing this.

Umm... Dhruv told me... he wanted to hear your voice, but it was past midnight, so he told me about your routine...

I'm sorry, Dhruv, but given the situation you have created, you deserve more punishment than the scolding Nidhi will give you once you get out of the hospital...

.

"You are mad, Dhruv"

....

Nidhi
Piyush: Medanta it is. We are shifting him to Medanta. It's already late, and you must sleep; it is already two hours from your sleeping time...

Huh! How did he know my routine? He needs to answer this...

How do you know my sleeping routine?
Answer quickly, Piyush... {tap... tap...} why isn't this piece of technology lighting up... {taping on the phone screen}
Beep... beep...
Piyush: - Umm... Dhruv told me... he wanted to hear your voice, but it was past midnight, so he told me about your

routine...

Why am I smiling? I should be worried, right? Dhruv knows my routine... but I feel no fear... I should stop smiling and need to go to sleep.

"You are mad, Dhruv"

22
Cut short

Next Day

Piyush

Doctor: The treatment he received is acceptable, and I am sure he has no internal injury...

[We reached Medanta early in the morning, and Dhruv was taken for multiple tests; after two hours, we met Doctor Abhishek Sharma, who prescribed more tests. Our whole day went by like this, and it was 9:30 when the Doctor asked us to meet in his cabin. Maa decided to stay outside Dhruv's room. Uncle was with me.]

But, sir, he was screaming in pain.

Doctor: - When?

He is just unconscious because of low energy and sedatives...

Kamal: - Mr. Sharma, yesterday night he was screaming and was uncontrollable...

["Where was he in those four days?" My uncle and the Doctor were busy discussing things, but I was thinking about those four days... then I started looking at reports]

I looked at the reports, but they were similar to earlier reports, and the Doctor and uncle were also confused.

But sir... before I could say further, **the nurse slammed the door and entered screaming, "Sir, sir, that patient in room no. 208 is screaming, and...** she was out of breath, so we quickly **got up, realizing it was Dhruv... and "maa" was there alone...**

Huff... huff... I ran as fast as I could but was low on breath upon reaching there.

Upon seeing us approaching the room, Maa hugged me. "Piyush, save Dhruv... Piyush... her breath was failing her... **uncle tried to control Maa. Today, I decided to enter the room with the Doctor...**

Doctor: - Dhruv, Calm down...

Dhruv: - Leave me alone... leave me... stop it... stop it... I can't do it...

I was shell-shocked seeing him like this... he had lost not only weight but also his muscles... he was screaming his lungs out... tears in his eyes... he was forcing his core so much...

Stop it, he screamed the loudest, and suddenly, he stopped moving and passed out, and a tear fell from his eyes, but why did I feel he looked at me before passing out...

For the first time in many days, I lost hope and felt helpless... I went near him, wiped his tears off, and started moving towards the gate... [my shoulder dropped]

What the hell would I say to "Maa."

Doctor: - why is he unclad?

Huh! Unclad... yesterday, too, he was unclad... [I stopped in my tracks as I heard it... there must be something related to his lower body]

Sir, he was screaming the same way as yesterday and was unclad. Is he possibly having some internal injury at the core or lower body?

Doctor: - possible... you go outside... we might need to take him for one more test...

Hmm sure...

Kamal: - Piyush...

Manju "maa": - what did the Doctor say?

Tears in a mother's eyes can break you completely... the way "maa" was clenching my shirt made me feel miserable...

"maa," calm down; the doctors have said they are taking him for another test...

Kamal: - what test?

Uncle, I think he has some injury in his core...

Kamal: - core? Why do you think so?

I narrated what I saw, and as I was narrating, fear gripped me. first, I saw "maa" falling on her knees... like a lifeless body... before I could do something... I saw Nidhi, and her face was pale white...

Uncle was trying to soothe "maa," but for the first time, I saw a tear in his eyes... I was sitting on an adjusting bench when Nidhi came and sat beside me...

Nidhi: - Where are his reports?

Piyush: - He will be alright... before I could say something... she yelled at me...

Nidhi: - Stop this nonsense...

Her voice caught everyone's attention, including Uncle...

Uncle, she is "Nidhi," our college friend... {how can this man smile even in so much pain... Dhruv, I will never forgive you... your father is truly a superhero} Uncle greeted him with namaste, but "maa" was still lost {felt like a lifeless body hanging by a thread of breath} Nidhi got up from the bench and folded her hands to greet uncle...

Nidhi: - I want the whole truth about the last three days. Stop with this nonsense and lie...

Her voice was low, but her intensity was fearsome...

I handed over his reports and tried to hide his screams and incidents. See yourself. Reports are regular. Don't worry, Nidhi.

Nidhi: - When I can slap Dhruv... you are more timid than him... don't you forget...

It was hurtful, but I agreed if she could slap Dhruv, I am nobody in front of her... but still, I said what do you mean?

Nidhi: - I heard his screams, I listened to his screams loud and clear... tell me the truth...

I went pale hearing her words... but decided to tell her the truth... "It has been a continuous occurrence for the last three days."

Nidhi: - continuous?

Yes, once a day and, more specifically, at night... This was the same reason we had to shift him overnight to Medanta. But it is 10 p.m., so why are you here?

Nidhi: - I wanted to see him...

Umm... I wanted to ask her... "why?" but his visual just before he got unconscious left me drained...

I was looking at the Doctor's office, waiting for the test result... Nidhi was still here... I asked her to go home as it was getting late, but she was adamant and asked me, "Can I see him?"

I said no, but she didn't oblige.

Nidhi: - I am going to see him...

I don't know what made Dhruv Love her so much..., but her eyes are enough to scare somebody. The intensity of her eyes and words is no match for any girl I have seen... scary stuff...

I followed her to Dhruv's room... and fear gripped her... I saw her backstepping a little...

Nidhi: - what the hell happened to him; he had lost so much weight, but his reports seem normal...

That is what doctors are trying to find.

Before we could move further...

Please don't come near me... don't do it... we heard his voice... but his eyes were closed... his body was shivering... he was yelling, but not the screams we heard earlier... I quickly called the Doctor... and they advised us to go out...

As soon as we got outside... "maa" came near me asking what happened, but fortunately, this time, I had Nidhi with me. She quickly controlled "maa" and soothed her by saying: Dhruv is trying to regain consciousness... that left me speechless, but "maa" got a smile on her face... so I remained silent.

I was quiet, but Nidhi understood. I wanted to know why she had lied.

Nidhi: - You boys don't understand a mother's heart... I know it was a lie, but it got his mother a sense, a will, and power to hold herself up and fight for his son... "no one is stronger than a mother for her children."

I nodded and thought about how much Dhruv would have loved seeing Nidhi and his mother together... I smiled a little... but...

"But my smile was cut short."

23

I shouldn't have let him go.

---❦---

Doctor: - Piyush, come in... Mr. Kamal, not you or anybody else, only Piyush.

I looked at my uncle and then at Nidhi... she yelled; go on, be quick.

[unable to process, why me only?] [And I wanted to say, Nidhi, I am closer to Dhruv, not you, but that would be a bad idea, so I entered the Doctor's cabin alone.]

Doctor: - Sit Piyush

Yes, sir, is everything okay with Dhruv?

Doctor: - Why didn't you tell me Dhruv has nocturnal emission?

Sorry, sir, but what is nocturnal emission?

Doctor: - Wet dreams.

Oh... [I realized what he was saying] but no, sir. I haven't heard him mention this... and honestly, he would not hide this from me. We have been together for years, and I haven't seen him taking any medicine related to this...

Doctor: - Are you sure?

Yes, sir. A thought gripped my mind before I could utter a word: "He was unclad." Sir, please tell me what's happening.

Doctor: - We found semen near his core, and it seemed it was released a few minutes ago...

I was in shock; I didn't say a word...

Doctor: - I am consulting my seniors... but it is way more complicated than it looks.

I was still in my thoughts when I left the Doctor's office, not realizing everyone was waiting for me... It felt like I was caged with monsters around me asking questions, but nothing was audible, and before I could say anything... I felt like throwing up, so I ran to the washroom and puked my heart out.

Uncle came running behind me, trying his best to help me. When I narrated what happened inside the Doctor's cabin... he went silent momentarily and asked me to lie before Maa.

Manju "maa": - you okay Piyush? Please take care of yourself. I can't see my sons like this.

I hug her and tell her it is an internal injury to Dhruv's Core, and he will be okay... [I lied, but my tears told Nidhi there was something else, but she remained quiet]

Nidhi: - What is it?

It is way more complicated than what we are thinking... [I narrated the whole conversation]

Nidhi went quiet, then she said, what was he screaming when we were in the room and before that when you were in the room...

"Stop it, don't come near to me, don't do it," and I think after his scream, he looked at me before passing out... like he wanted to tell me something.

Nidhi: - But who was he trying to stop? I can understand the scream in pain, but "stop it," "don't come near me."

"What happened to him in those four days?" Did somebody beat him up?

Nidhi: - You have seen him brawling. Even when drunk, his strength would have taken at least two men down, if not more. And what is the explanation for his lost weight?

"I shouldn't have let him go... "

24
Please take me away

The following day, I woke up with a mild headache. I need medicine for this headache. But first, let me ask Nidhi whether she reached home safely last night.

Before I could text her, I received her call.

Nidhi: - I am at college, so I won't be able to come today, but if you need anything, give me a call...

I will...

Nidhi: - How's Dhruv?

Still unconscious...

Nidhi: - You need to do one thing. You told me he screams at night. You need to make sure Aunty doesn't hear that tonight...

I will... before I could say anything else... chaos erupted in the hospital; wardens were running towards a room.

"Help me, save me... a shrilling scream of a girl caught everyone off-guard, and realizing it was coming from Dhruv's Room, I ran inside his room, and it left me terrified."

I tried to ensure Maa didn't see this, but I was late... "Dhruv was holding a surgical knife, and four wardens were trying to control him as he was trying to stab the nurse... I was shocked, but realizing I had to act fast, I quickly jumped *in and tried to calm him, but it seemed he was hell-bent on stabbing her."*

The Doctor called for an injection, and another nurse took that nurse out. Upon injecting, he became unconscious again...

But as soon as I turned around, I saw both uncle and aunty sitting on the floor with their face blank and tears flowing...

This sight broke both uncle and aunty to the core... I tried to soothe them but to no avail. We all moved when the Doctor called us, but our eyes still struck on Dhruv.

Before the Doctor could say anything, I apologized for the incident. Uncle Aunty was still completely lost, sitting in the chair opposite the Doctor...

Doctor: - It's okay, Piyush. But for my staff's safety, I have to take some measures and...

Measures? And?

Doctor: - Measure as in, we have to tie his hands...

A shock went through my spine.

Doctor: - only male staff near him... and we need to take him for a CT scan, and I need to consult a psychiatrist...

For the second time in a few minutes... I felt my legs would give up... before I could say something...

Do whatever you feel like, Doctor. I want my son to be okay, said the uncle, his hand folded like a helpless father pleading for his son.

I was not furious anymore with Dhruv. I was disheartened and just wanted him back...

When I came out with Uncle and Aunty, I realized I didn't disconnect the call... I prayed to God before looking at the phone [she must have or should have disconnected the call]

But my day got worse as I saw the call was still active... I fall to the bench before saying, "Hello."

Nidhi: - I heard everything,
Complete silence followed those words...
Nidhi: We should find out what happened to him in those four days... You can't do anything about the earlier plan, "Aunty will not leave Dhruv's side after this incident."
I want my brother back... [tear rolled down from my eyes]
Nidhi: - don't give up, Piyush; I don't want to Give up yet...

.

.

.

I looked at the watch, and it was 9:30 p.m.... another fear gripped me. I went near my uncle and asked him to come with me, but...
Manju "maa": - I will not leave, and don't worry, Piyush, I know he will be screaming in a few minutes...
Seeing "maa" stone eyes and hearing those words broke me... uncle sat down again in anticipation of Dhruv's Scream... it felt like my soul had left my body. I sat down with them, and as soon as I saw Nidhi approaching us... Dhruv's Scream startled us...
"don't do this to me... stop it..."
Nidhi quickly reached and sat beside "maa," holding her tight as we heard Dhruv scream...

.

"Kill me... Take me away..."

These words sent shivers to all of us...

.

"Take me away."

25

Don't harm her

Nidhi

[Piyush: - I was looking at Maa, who lost her charm by looking at Dhruv like this; it felt that Maa got old by five years in four days; eyes sunken in, shoulder dropped.]

Piyush, where is the CT scan report?

Piyush: - Its normal... The doctor is waiting for him to regain consciousness so we can consult a psychiatrist.

Piyush, I am sorry... I never thought you would have to see this day because of my careless words...

Piyush: - It's not your fault. I am angry with him, but my boy fell in love with the right girl... and truly meant it when he said, "he is in love with you."

Umm...

Piyush: - You are here taking care of his mother when you are not obliged to do it... and that reason is enough for me to understand that "he was right in choosing you" and stop saying it was your fault. It's his fault, only his fault, for whatever situation we are in and he is in.

Piyush, we must find out what happened to him in those four days.

Piyush: - once he regains his consciousness and we get a report from a psychiatrist...

Umm... okay, I will leave. Something surprising is happening for our class tomorrow. I wanted to stay, but the principal instructed everyone to be present in college tomorrow... so I have to leave...

Piyush: - Not an issue... stay safe, and don't forget to text upon reaching home...

I was about to leave when a thought struck my mind... "Where is Dhruv's Mobile?"

Piyush: - It's with me...

He took Dhruv's mobile from his pocket, and I took it from him and sat back. He was perplexed but didn't utter a word...

It is password protected...

Piyush: - type your name...

Now I am in shock... and to add to it, I saw my picture as his wallpaper. It was from our annual day in the third year... I looked at Piyush, but he didn't utter a word...

Empty messages? Piyush, why is there no message on his phone...

Piyush: - I don't know; he might have deleted it to free up some space.

Space? It looks like he likes to click pictures. The gallery folder occupies most of the phone's space...

Piyush: - umm, don't open it...

Okay, you didn't stop me from looking at his phone, but what's with the gallery... I need to look into it, and shh...

Okay, what the hell is this... why do I find my pics in his phone, and what's with this editing... kinemaster, picsart... there are 1000s of my pictures...

Piyush: He used to edit your pictures whenever he missed you. He used to say, "It's my way of expressing how I see her, what color I want to fill in our life."

Can I take his mobile with me?

Piyush: - but why? *[perplexed expression written over his face]*

I want to look at his editing... but will you say no? I don't think so... I smirked at him *[I just took the benefit of being loved by Dhruv]...*

Bye bye, Piyush...

.

.

.

Dhruv
What have I done?

"DON'T LET HER TAME YOU"

What have you done, Dhruv?

Please leave me alone. I am sorry... I can't fold my hands.

Shh... shh... you are mine... I will give you everything you want in life... hahahahaha... *[It's the same tone as I heard when she appeared for the first time]*

I want to be free. Please leave me alone... before I could say something, she bit me on the lips and whispered in my ear... "you are mine," and I see a girl outside whom you call Nidhi... if you try to go near her, I will kill her...

hahahahaha...

no, no, don't harm her or my mother...

shh... you are mine...

"Don't harm her."

26

A ray of hope

Students, I am happy to see everyone present today... professor quips...

Nidhi

Dhruv! I am sorry... but now I understand it was not an attraction you felt for me. Not only the edits, but I realized you used to write small stories for me... Damm, Dhruv, why didn't you express yourself in this way?

And why on earth I am at college rather than at the hospital?

Why is everyone excited? Especially girls...

Parul, why are these girls so excited?

Parul: - are you serious? You don't know...

Know what?

Parul: - its...

Professor: - please give a round of applause for Mr. Viren Arora...

Viren Arora... that famous psychiatrist

.

.

.

.

Viren Arora
Hi guys,
Nidhi: As soon as he said "hi," all the girls were screaming like they saw a movie actor... To his credit, he is also pretty famous for his looks.

Well, I am overwhelmed by your reaction, but I promise I won't take much of your time...

You can have all of our time if you want to... a girl's voice led to another round of hooting...

I am flattered, but I want to discuss something that I feel you need to be aware of... so I request everyone to have some patience...

Nowadays, children are afraid to tell their parents how they feel, and that's a big mistake... especially for college-going kids...

But I understand it is not easy to share everything with your parents, so I suggest you find a person, friend, or professional to seek help and share rather than committing something harmful to yourself and your parents...

And nowadays, I see a trend where kids believe in tantric... paranormal entities... I request you all to stay away from these kinds of activities. It can be fatal for you, and it can exhaust you mentally...

.

.

Dhruv
Umm... ouch... why am I being tied?
Warden: - you are awake...
Umm... why am I being tied? Free my hands...
Warden: - I should call the Doctor immediately.
Where are you going? Untie my hands first.
Warden: - Doctor, Doctor...

Piyush: - why is he running? Wait, let me follow him, Uncle and Aunty. You stay here...

Doctor: - Piyush! He is awake... but you will not enter the room till the psychiatrist reports...

Manju "Maa": - But why? I want to meet my son...

Doctor: Mr. Kamal, please understand that we need to be sure he is completely fine before we let you meet him. Please don't forget how he reacted the last time he woke up... I hope you understand...

Kamal: - I do, please look after my son...

Doctor, Sir, why am I being tied like this? I am not an animal.

Doctor: - Calm down, Dhruv... it was a necessity. I will tell you everything, but first, let me look at you and let us do some required tests...

More tests?

.

.

.

Nidhi

Viren Arora: I hope you all understand. Now I would like to inform you all... you don't have to hear my blabbering anymore.

He seems to be a nice guy. I have heard from his patients, but seeing and hearing him today, I feel everyone was right about him.

Can I talk to him about Dhruv's situation... will he help me?

There's no point in thinking. Nidhi, go for it... I raised my hand and said, Sir...

[everyone is looking at me. Ignore them.]

Sir, you said we can consult an expert, but how?

Viren: If you know an expert or professional, go for it without hesitation. If you ask them not to tell your family or anybody, they will protect your privacy...

But what if we don't know a professional?

Viren: Well, you know me now. Here is my secretary. She will help you. Book an appointment whenever anyone feels like...

But what if it's an emergency?

He looked at me with his curious eyes before speaking...

Viren: - mam, please set up a 2-chair arrangement in the garden...

If anybody wants to discuss something, please join me in the garden...

I raised my hand and said; I want to discuss something...

Viren: - be my guest miss...

Nidhi...

Viren: - Miss. Nidhi

.

.

Dhruv

Why am I still tied, Doctor?

Doctor: A senior doctor is coming to meet you. Here he is, "Mr. Lalwani."

Mr. Lalwani: - how are you feeling, Dhruv?

Tired and more pissed off at being tied...

Mr. Lalwani: Oh, don't worry. It's just a few more minutes. If you feel comfortable, can I ask you some questions?

.

.

Nidhi

Viren: - So, Miss Nidhi, what do you want to discuss?

Are you sure, Nidhi, you want to do this...

Viren: I can read that you feel awkward; it's written on your face. But I promise it will be beneficial.

I sighed in relief before narrating everything that transpired in the last few days... I could see he was sincerely listening to me and engrossed with what I said...

Viren: - where is he right now?

Medanta hospital...

Viren: - and what time you said, he starts screaming...

At 10 in the evening...

Viren: - and what did the psychiatrist say?

They are waiting for him to wake up... he calls his secretary and says, "We are going to Medanta at 9:30 in the evening."

Viren: I will meet him today and let you and his parents know how I feel... I would appreciate it if I met you there...

Sure, I will be there... Thank you so much... [I got excited]

Viren: - I love to help people...

.

.

.

Dhruv

Please untie my hands...

Mr. Lalwani: - last question, I promise...

As he was about to question me, I saw somebody entering the room... "a girl," "a nurse."

And fear gripped my mind.

"I will kill every girl who tries to come near you." Her words and laughter started circling my mind...

Tell her to leave, I yelled... tell her to leave...

Seeing me getting impatient, she fumbled the plate she was carrying...

But I can't let her harm anybody... I yelled again, telling her to leave this room right now... no female should enter my room... I cried harder, I screamed at her...

Mr. Lalwani: She is going Dhruv. Calm down. Please leave the room nurse right now.

I don't know when I passed out, but the last word that I blurred looking at her leaving the room was...

"No female should enter the room."

27

Isheok

Nidhi

Where is Piyush? Mr. Viren will be here anytime. I must tell him, his Uncle, and his Aunt about this.

[I looked around outside Dhruv's room, but they were nowhere to be found. I moved a little forward and saw them sitting together on the far bench.]

Here he is with his uncle and aunt, but why are they so dull?

Piyush...

Piyush: - Nidhi, umm, how are you?

I am OK, but why are you sounding so dull... is he OK?

Piyush: Let us move to that bench. It is more complicated than we thought. He woke up in the morning, but...

But what? Don't create the suspense.

Piyush: - it was all going well. The psychiatrist was pretty happy with what he was hearing, but suddenly, he started yelling at the nurse to leave the room... he was aggressive, he was yelling, and before he passed out, he said, "No female should enter this room."

What the hell? What the... wait, so that means Aunty is not allowed to meet him?

Piyush: - nobody is allowed to meet him...

Don't you worry, I will be allowed to meet him...

A voice startled Piyush and... I looked up and found Mr. Viren standing... I quickly got up and introduced Piyush to him, narrating our conversation.

Piyush: - [still perplexed] let me take you to his father and mother...

Viren: - Hi, Mr. Kamal, I am Viren Arora... a psychiatrist

Kamal: I have heard about you. But is my son so sick that you have to visit him?

Listening to this, Dhruv's mother got up and clenched Dhruv's father's hand...

Viren: - No, No... I visited Bihani College today and learned about your son from Nidhi... I must say your son is one lucky kid to have friends like Piyush and Nidhi. Please be seated.

I watched him talking to the doctors who treated Dhruv... aunty came to me and gave me a forehead kiss... Piyush looked out of his senses... but everything stopped when we heard Dhruv Screaming...

But Mr. Viren stopped everyone from going inside the room. He looked at Dhruv from the window... and asked Piyush to keep a tab on the duration and compare it to the earlier days...

I was in shock, but no one protested. Uncle and Aunty sat there helpless, utterly dependent on whatever the doctor said, "just wishing that their son would be fine one day." "kill me... Take me away..." These were his last words before the scream died down and he became unconscious...

Mr. Viren let the Doctors enter the room, sat down near Piyush, and asked her secretary to set up a meeting with Mr. Lalwani and Mr. Sharma.

Viren: - Piyush, what do you think the duration of today was similar to earlier days?

Piyush: - yes, pretty similar...

Viren: So that means it was not the medicine controlling him. He stopped screaming after a certain period every day...

We all stared at him because of what he said, and then we realized he was not wrong, but I wanted to hear more from him...

Viren: I don't think it's an internal injury, but let's all wait for the doctor's report. Once I get it, I will meet Dhruv...

Can you tell us? "What's your first assessment?" I quipped...

If not a head injury, it can be many mental disorders, for starters, but let me talk to him once, and then I will let you all know...

28
Heard a podcast

Piyush

Looking at "maa" like this is tiring, but today is a big day as Mr. Viren will meet Dhruv... I should call Nidhi and ask her whether she Is coming or not.

Nidhi: - Hi, Piyush

It seems you are on your way to somewhere...

Nidhi: - Yes, I am going to college. I have talked with Mr. Viren's secretary. He will be at the hospital any minute... so you take care of everything. I will be there after college...

Okay, I think Mr. Viren is here... I will let you know everything...

Nidhi: - You should, and as soon as you get the words from Mr. Viren...

I smiled as I hung up the call. "Nidhi is way more engrossed with Dhruv's situation than she thinks."

Oh, Mr. Viren is with Mr. Lalwani. I should inform Uncle and "maa."

Viren: - No, No... I am coming; don't disturb Uncle and Aunty...

How did he know?

Viren: Hello, Piyush. Let us meet Dhruv's Parents, and then you will accompany me to Dhruv's Room...

I was still shocked when Mr. Viren greeted Uncle and "Maa" so warmly... I thought he might be the right one to cure Dhruv...

Viren: - Piyush, come here...

Huh! Sure...

Viren: I don't think it is an injury... I hope he tells us what exactly he is feeling, or we might need the police to investigate the missing four days. That might be the missing piece of the puzzle for the screams we hear from him...

I looked at Uncle, and he was calm. The only thing he wants right now is Dhruv's well-being...

Viren: - Where is Nidhi?

She is at college...

Viren: - Come with me,

Sure...

Viren: - Nidhi could be a reason for Dhruv's condition... don't get me wrong, but he yelled at a nurse, "No female should enter the room," so we can't ignore that angle...

I understand, but let us not say this in front of her...

Viren: - sure, let us meet Dhruv now...

.

.

.

We entered the room, but the Doctor told me to stay behind Mr. Viren. I did the same.

Viren: - Dhruv, Dhruv...

Dhruv: - Who is it? Umm... who are you now? Don't speak a word; first, ask them to untie me...

I controlled my tears, looking at Dhruv's face... he had lost his Charm... his hair seemed dead... his eyes sunken in... loss of weight reflected on his cheeks...

Viren: - Untie him! He ordered an attendant... and commanded him to leave after this...

I looked at Dhruv... he didn't utter a word and blurred out I need a beer... it was one of the most disgusting sentences I have heard from him... like seriously, his parents are losing their health and sleep over him, and he wants a beer...

Viren: - The hospital would not allow it, but I have an idea. You help me to cure yourself, and outside the hospital, we can have more than one beer at a time...

Dhruv: - Who are you? What do you want? Nobody can help me, I fucked up...

He fucked up? What the hell is he talking about?

Viren: - Try me...

Dhruv: - Where is Piyush?

Viren: - Piyush, come here.

As I got up from the couch, I saw him trying to get up, but Mr. Viren stopped him...

Dhruv: - Piyush! I fucked up...

I wanted to scold him, but seeing the tears in his eyes, I felt helpless... what did you do, Dhruv?

Dhruv: - i... i... I fucked up...

Viren: - how?

Dhruv got agitated and said who are you... just go away...

Dhruv, He is Mr. Viren. Please tell us what happened to you. We will help you, man. And don't say anybody can not help you.

He remained silent, but Mr. Viren didn't move an inch. He handed the tablets to him and looked after him without any hesitation... and when I felt agitated, he calmed me but didn't pressure Dhruv for one second. He calmly waited for Dhruv to feel comfortable...

Dhruv: - Piyush, I want to tell you everything, but she might hear us...

Who's she?

He again went silent, but this time, Mr. Viren made a move...

Viren: - We have a whole day, Dhruv. We can have this awkward silence for an entire day, but one thing is sure: You are not leaving this bed or hospital without letting us know what is happening to you.

I asked Dhruv one more time... "Who's she?"

"karnapisachani"

What the hell did you say? As soon as he said this, my mind went to the podcast we heard on Nidhi's B'day...

You have lost your mind? What the hell are you talking about?

Viren: - calm down, Piyush, have a seat... Dhruv, Who's She? And tell me everything in detail...

"karnapisachani"

"All this started when I heard that podcast."

29

As soon as we left the room, we saw Nidhi with Uncle and Aunty...

Before they could question me, Mr. Viren came to my Rescue...

Viren: - It's more of a mental trauma, but I will provide you more details once I finish my assessment. I will take a leave and soon let you know the measures and things we must do.

Saying this, he started moving, and I thought I was doomed, but he is one gem of a person.

Viren: - I don't think it is an injury... I hope he tells us precisely what he is feeling, or we might need the police to investigate the four days he is missing. That might be the missing piece of the puzzle for the screams we hear from him...

Hearing this, everyone got relaxed...

But what I heard inside that room was too much to take. I need to throw it out right now. I excused myself for a while...

.

.

Dhruv narrated the whole story. I have no emotion left for that man. How can someone be so dumb? He just let an *illusion take over his mind, and look at him now... fighting for his life from a lever infection...*

And how in the world did he eat his own... yuck, I am puking just at the thought of it...

And for what? Power? What power was he looking for? What the hell was he thinking?

....

Viren

Listen, everyone... no more appointments. Order a coffee for me, and you can all take a leave for today...

["karnapisachani" all started when I heard a podcast...
I wanted the power. I tried to succeed. My anger and hatred for my condition made me overlook all the consequences...
I ate ... ... drank ... ... and I wasn't able to control my urge when she came near me and I fucked up everything...
Every day, she wants me to fulfill her sexual desire; she wants chicken and alcohol, and that's why I scream stop it...]

He made many mistakes, and it seems it has taken over his mind... he thinks she has taken over his body, and the information given to him has occupied his mind...

But that screams and semen and him being unclad... what could it be?

I need to research thoroughly, or he might harm himself or some other unintentionally...

First, I need to look into that podcast and "karnapisachani."

[tantric: - two things I want to convey, which is on arisen in youth, black magic to kill somebody and "karnapisachani"]

What bull shit are they selling to the people of this city... its utter crap... let me make a mental note; the first thing I need to do tomorrow morning is to ask the authority to take down this episode...

[Karnapisachani is a Sadhana with the help of which negative entities around us are controlled and made to work. There are positive and negative entities (spirits) roaming around us. Since managing the positive energies can be difficult, maintaining the negative energies can still be accessible. However, it is easy for only those who know how to complete the Sadhana without letting the hurdles disturb the entire process. A Sadhak must know how to complete the Sadhana.

The entities that are used to get the work done through the Karnapisachani process are lusty, have high sexual powers, and can do anything to have their sexual thirst fulfilled.]

Why in the hell are the boys fascinated by this information? After his treatment, I should organize a seminar for boys...

So, he manifested an entity, and now he thinks she is controlling him, and he is her slave... he is not possessed; he is her slave according to him...

.

.

.

Schizophrenia

[persistent delusions: the person has fixed beliefs that something is true, despite evidence to the contrary; persistent hallucinations: the person may hear, smell, see, touch, or feel things that are not there; experiences of influence, control, or passivity: the experience that one's feelings, impulses, actions, or thoughts are not generated by oneself, are being placed in one's mind or withdrawn from one's mind by others, or that one's thoughts are being broadcast to others;]

.

I have to consider his family until he gets over it, and I might have to tell Nidhi about it because there is no way she would not try to meet Dhruv in the upcoming days. That can be fatal for both of them...

It's already 9 o'clock. I should meet them in the morning and hope Piyush will forget what he heard today...

....

Piyush

Nidhi: - what is the actual matter Piyush?

Huh! *[I was feeling like I was sitting here after smoking weed for a whole day. Emotions, fear, and empathy for him were gone.]*

Nidhi: - I know you are hiding something from me...

I can tell you for sure that he fucked up badly... and if you believe in Mr. Viren, then there is a chance else we have lost him...

Nidhi: - what the hell are you saying?

What time is it? *[My emotions towards him vanished]*

Nidhi: Huh! It's 9:35. Oh, I won't lie. This is the most painful hour...

Not really... I stood up before she could ask me anything more...

Nidhi: - You have time until morning to tell me what exactly happened with him in those four days... I know he told you everything...

She said it in a calming tone that could send shivers down your spine. Her aura in our class was unmatched...

I was still in my thoughts when we heard Dhruv's Scream... but today, it was different. He did not yell a word; he said only one sentence...

"Take me away."

I looked at him from the window. It was similar to other days... he was unclad, and he yelled once more before passing out...

I went inside the room to clean him... I will never forgive him, but I will not leave his side when he needs...

....

Dhruv

Umm... Piyush, listen... I grabbed his hand when he was about to leave...

Piyush: - leave my hand...

I know you are angry, but listen to me once...

Piyush: - I don't want to listen to anything you want to say.

Please, listen to me...

Piyush: - umm... okay, say it. What crap do you want to speak? You tortured her, me, and yourself earlier, but now you tortured your family too...

I presented a smile because I knew he was right...

Piyush: - everything is fun for you...

Please never leave "maa" alone... I said it with tears in my eyes, and that might have irked him more... he grabbed my collar... but he didn't punch me...

Please listen to me once, Piyush. I don't have much time... {I saw a tear in his eyes. This man truly cared for me as a brother}

Piyush: - say what you want to say.

I am sorry for everything... because of me, everyone is facing so much... but I am sure it will end soon... she will take me away... {shh... shh...} don't interrupt... promise me you will take care of maa and papa...

Piyush: - I wanted to kill him, but for the first time in weeks, I have seen guilt in his eyes... he is not pretending... why the hell did you do it, Dhruv?

Promise me...

Piyush: - nothing will happen to you...

Shh... shh... promise me, I don't want to hear anything else...

Piyush: - I promise... stop getting anxious, I am right here...

.

.

Manju "maa": - what did he say?

Umm... I was in my thoughts that I forgot; everyone was waiting outside for me...

I wanted to lie, but I just broke down at the thought of losing Dhruv... I hugged Maa and lied while in tears, "he will be fine, for sure."

"He will be fine, will he?"

30

I want my answers

---♡---

Secretary: - sir, patients are calling for the appointment...

Not today, I am leaving for Medanta...

Secretary: - sir, everything okay?

Not really; college kids are doomed. But first, connect me to the stakeholders of the Param podcast...

Secretary: - Param podcast?

Yes

Secretary: - okay, give me a minute...

Be quick. I need to leave for Medanta...

Secretary: - Sir, Mr. Param is on line no. 5

Hello, Mr. Param... I would love it if you pull down episode no. 18 {tantric}. It's related to my work and one of my patients, and I don't want to take any legal route. So, I request you to please take down that episode right now.

.

Miss. Roshni: - please look after it, follow up efficiently, and I am leaving...

Secretary: - yes, sir...

.

Hello, Mr. Lalwani

Hello, Piyush... wait here... let me get the blessing from Uncle and Aunty first and call Nidhi... tell her to be here...

Is Dhruv awake, Piyush?

Piyush: - yes, sir.

Uncle and Aunty, I have found Dhruv's problem and know what treatment is required.

Let me meet him once, and then I want you all at the canteen... Mr. Lalwani, you too...

.

Hello Dhruv,

Dhruv: - Umm... hello sir,

Oh my god, you are a handsome boy with a pretty smile... how are you?

Dhruv: - sir, I am not lying...

And why do you think that I don't believe you? And shh... shh... I am here to know. Is there anything else I should know?

Dhruv: - I told you everything.

Good, now rest up. I will meet you in an hour...

.

.

Piyush, where are Nidhi, Uncle, and Aunty?

Nidhi: - Hello, sir,

Everyone, we should move to the canteen and don't you worry, he is sleeping...

Piyush: - If you want me to stay here, I will. *[I tried my best to avoid the situation and aftereffects from Nidhi and Dhruv's parents]*

No, everybody in the canteen...

[Piyush: - Before i try one more time]

Manju "maa": - Piyush, shh... do as he says... and no more question...

.

.

Mr. Lalwani, prepare his discharge orders...
Nidhi: - What?
Yes, medicines can heal his liver. But for mental health, we need to do many things that are not possible in these surroundings...

He has Schizophrenia... in simple terms, he manifested something, and now he is hallucinating the same...

Before you ask me something, he is my patient now. I will not share every detail with you until I feel it is necessary...

You have to trust me completely: I will heal him... your son will be fine...

Uncle: - What do we have to do?

Go to Hanumangarh. Let me present you with the complete procedure and measures we must take...

{rehab, counseling, medication}

We will start with medication and counseling, and when his situation gets a little better, we will work on his rehab.

And now, what should we take care of?

As I already mentioned, Uncle and Aunty, you will leave for Hanumangarh; Piyush, you will shift with him; and Nidhi, you will not meet him till I say...

Piyush: - I want my brother to be okay. I accept...

He seems to have a grip on himself. He is a pretty reliable guy with a mature head on his shoulder.

Nidhi: - But why can't I meet him, and why can't he stay with Uncle and Aunty?

You have to believe in me...

Nidhi: - Shut up! I like a prominent answer...

Piyush: - Okay, Nidhi is one fearless girl, but this was not a way to talk with Mr. Viren, and not to mention Uncle and Aunty are still here...

Mr. Lalwani, please prepare the discharge paper...
Mr. Lalwani: - Sure...

Nidhi, I like your desperation, but that is why I want you to stay away from him...

Nidhi: - As I said, I would like a prominent answer.

Piyush: - Here comes his cold eyes attitude... I am not interfering at any cost...

I wanted to hide this detail, but seeing your expression, I don't think you will allow me...

Nidhi: - pretty much the jest of it...

Okay, what is Schizophrenia?

Nidhi: - You want me to google it?

No, no... calm down a little, Miss Nidhi... Schizophrenia is a mental disorder in which a person gets

[persistent delusions: the person has fixed beliefs that something is true, despite evidence to the contrary;

persistent hallucinations: the person may hear, smell, see, touch, or feel things that are not there;

experiences of influence, control, or passivity: the experience that one's feelings, impulses, actions, or thoughts are not generated by oneself, are being placed in one's mind or withdrawn from one's mind by others, or that one's thoughts are being broadcast to others;]

Nidhi: - Still, I haven't received my answer. And Piyush, stop looking at Uncle and Aunty...

Piyush: - umm... *[I looked at Mr. Viren, but he was still smiling]*

He thinks he is in the control of a negative entity, "karnapisachani."

Piyush: - those words echoed in my ears, and all I could muster from the situation is that Nidhi and "maa" expressions changed Dramatically, and Uncle tried hard not to give away anything... Complete silence for minutes, followed by Mr. Viren trying to narrate his plans...

I don't know much about the entity, but Dhruv's reaction towards a nurse earlier and then during his counseling with Mr. Lalwani, I think it is best for him that we keep him away from Aunty and Nidhi...

Nidhi: - What exactly did he say During his counseling with Mr. Lalwani...

Piyush: - umm... [her eyes stoned, face down, tone minimal but intensity still high] ... **"No female should enter this room."**

Nidhi: - so, he was trying to protect her, and now he is trying to protect Aunty and me...

What do you mean, Nidhi?

Nidhi: - what I read on the internet... {dark web to be particular}.

"If you have "karnapisachani" in your life, you won't be able to get close to any other girl... even to your mother, sister... "IF YOU DO, IT WOULD BE FATAL"

Manju "maa": - I want my son back... I will do anything and everything as you say. Just save my son...

Nidhi: - But who put that stuff in his mind?

Kamal: - I will pay the bill, and then we will leave... I trust you, Mr. Viren...

Nidhi: - I want my answers before this treatment begins...

Kamal: - God bless you, Nidhi Beta. We are leaving now, and you can decide about him on our behalf...

"I want my answers."

31
Promise

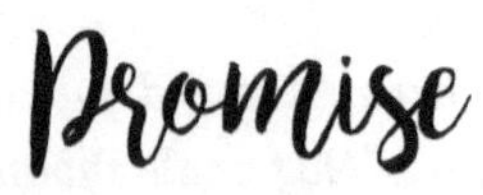

Piyush

Can we wait till "maa" leaves...

{Nidhi was in my ears. She was demanding her answers and explanation from me}

Nidhi: - you can't divert my mind?

Viren: - I will not do anything without your permission, I promise...

.

.

.

Nidhi, can I have a minute?

Nidhi: - No, first, tell me the whole story. And why didn't you tell me this earlier?

Viren: - calm down, Nidhi

Nidhi: - I believed in you, Mr. Viren

Viren: - Don't go on my smile; look at Piyush's face... I will tell you everything, but you must promise not to blame yourself...

Nidhi: - I am not promising you anything...

Nidhi, calm *{before I could complete the sentence, she stared at me, and my soul warned me}*

I'm sorry, Viren sir, but I know nothing. He told you everything... I am not ready to face her wrath...

Viren: - I will tell her everything, but she needs to calm down first...

.

.

.

Viren

Listen, Nidhi, now you know everything, but it is not your fault...

Nidhi: - it doesn't matter whose fault it is; I want him to be completely fine...

Then listen to me; you both need to help me...

Piyush, you will shift with Dhruv... and you will only stop him from liquor {only liquor, I mean} ... you will leave him alone when he starts screaming...

Nidhi, you will only contact Piyush or me and...

Nidhi: - and?

I might ask Dhruv to play Along with his mind...

Nidhi: - elaborate...

I will ask him to succumb to "karnapisachani" till I find a way out...

Nidhi: - What?

To calm him and stop that screaming... it's all in his mind, so we know there is nothing to worry about externally... subsequently, I will start his medication and counseling.

Nidhi: - But what if his hallucination becomes frequent?

To stop that from happening, we have medication... and to make him believe it is all in his mind, we will follow a counseling procedure...

Piyush: - Sir, have you ever encountered this type of case?

It's not the same, but I have seen people thinking they are possessed, but it always turns out to be anxiety...

Nidhi: - but in Dhruv's case, you are claiming it is Schizophrenia

Yes, the reason is "wet dreams." Please don't get confused; I don't think he has it, but I am not ready to leave any aspect unclosed...

Nidhi: - When are you planning to start the treatment?

Right now...

Nidhi: - Sorry?

I will meet Dhruv right now... and tell him I am seeking a solution. He has to succumb to her demands... and Nidhi, you must leave...

Nidhi: - Okay, but remember to inform me everything, Piyush...

Piyush: - umm... yes.

Nidhi: - Take care...

Piyush, you complete the remaining formalities. I am going to Dhruv's Room...

.

.

.

Dhruv, Dhruv... wake up.

Dhruv: - Who is this?

Viren,

come on, get up... you are getting discharged...

Dhruv: - huh! Ouch...

Yes, get up. I have something for you... I have been reading about "karnapisachani"

Dhruv: - what?

Yes, there is a way out of it... but you need to follow my instructions...

Dhruv: - what instructions?

You will not leave your house without my permission...

Dhruv: - yes, but I have to eat chicken and drink alcohol to fulfill her desire...

I have a solution for this too... I will give you some medicine so you won't need alcohol and eat chicken as much as you want...

Dhruv: - but what about her sexual desire?

Umm... you are a young man; how does she look?

Dhruv: - huh?

How does she look?

Dhruv: - lusty...

Hmm, I like your smile. Then fulfill her desire until I find a way out... I know you are perplexed by this, but it is just a time-buying technique. Once we find a way out, you will be free...

Dhruv: - but...

You have to trust me...

Dhruv: - will I be free from her?

Yes...

"I will be free from her."

"I want him completely fine."

32
one life

—♡—

Dhruv
Will he be able to help me? I don't know, but I want to be free... I want to meet my mother, Nidhi, and apologize to her. I will do as he says...
Please save me...

.

.

.

Piyush
I hope we are not making a mistake... I don't want to lose my brother...

.

.

.

Nidhi
I want Dhruv back... please save him, Mr. Viren.

.

.

.

.

Viren

I need to be careful with him.... The good part is that he wants to live. Stay strong, Dhruv...

.

.

.

One situation, life on the line, many thoughts, and trust are all they can do...

Part 2

33

I have a plan

15 days later, Saturday evening

Viren

Knock... knock...

Piyush, Dhruv...

Piyush: - yes sir, please come in...

Please keep it in the refrigerator...

Piyush: - Sir, beer?

Dhruv: - huh! Beer, Viren...

Piyush: - Dhruv, viren? [show some respect] Viren sir...

Calm down, Piyush. He is a friend... Dhruv, I am against cigarettes. So, leave the cigarettes and give us a minute. We will be back...

Piyush, come with me...

Piyush: - yes, sir...

Call Nidhi...

Piyush: - huh!

And call Uncle, too. But before that, tell me what you have observed these last 15 days.

Piyush: - he stopped screaming. He is happy, but sometimes, he talks about something unseen.

Piyush, tell me, do you feel there is an improvement?

Piyush: He hopes he will be okay someday; he considers her a friend now...

I told him to do it...

Piyush: - but I am afraid, sorry to say, sir, but nothing substantial improvement...

I know that's why I have come up with a plan...

Piyush: - What plan?

Call Nidhi and ask her to meet us tomorrow...

"I have a plan."

34
Worth a try

Saturday, morning...

Miss Roshni...

Secretary: - yes sir...

Cancel all the appointments...

Secretary: - sure, sir, but can I ask you something, sir... if you don't mind?

Miss Roshni, I am not in the mood to tell you why I am canceling all the appointments...

Secretary: - sir, you always say, "It is good to share"

Haha... very efficient... okay have a seat, but first, cancel all the appointments and order 2 cups of coffee...

Secretary: - done sir...

Pick up that red file. "This is the case for which I visited Medanta."

.

.

.

Secretary: - what the hell? Sorry for my language, but how is this possible?

The significant concern is that nothing is working on him. There has been no improvement, and his friends and family *have shown their trust in me...*

Secretary: - umm... so that's why you called Mr. Param that day...

Yes, the only good thing happening these days is his will to live is increasing significantly.

Secretary: - sir, why don't you look for something unorthodox?

As in?

Secretary: - don't get me wrong, sir... but why don't we use mythical ways in this case?

Elaborate... *[I sat down and was curious to know]*

Secretary: Sir, he went to a tantric, and now he feels he is in control of a hostile entity. So why don't we seek the help of a tantric?

Huh! Tantric?

Secretary: - yes, sir, can I use your laptop...

Sure, go on...

Secretary: - sir, look at it...

The concept of exorcism found in Abrahamic cultures drastically differs from the Vedic Hindu perspective.

In Hinduism, we know that people "possessed" by hostile spirits are troubled by "hungry ghosts" who are stuck between dimensions and unable to enter the dynamic of reincarnation due to some severe karmic problem. Therefore, they are LESS POWERFUL than human beings and try to suck the energy of the human and use their body to perform actions they would not be able to do otherwise.

Hinduism offers the solution to APPEASE (tarpana) the poor, confused, and suffering soul by elevating its level of consciousness, presenting sacred water (usually from Ganga), sanctified food (pinda, etc.), and reciting the glorification of divine Personalities of Godhead from Puranas, etc. It is not an act of war but compassion comparable to the recently developed *"secular" concept of "ghost whisperer."*

In Hindu tradition, there are rituals to oppose demonic forces, but they are fundamentally different because they do not involve a "possessed" human.

Such demonic forces are not interested in possessing the body of a poor human being, as these demonic beings are, by nature, much more potent than mere human beings. For them, trying to possess the body of a puny human would be like an eagle trying to ride a bicycle to move around - it would just make no sense.

I believe that the "evil spirit" in "demonic possession" cases among Abrahamics are very angry (not just hungry) ghosts of deceased Abrahamic believers, who after death, have discovered that they had been very wrong in their behavior and choices during their previous life, and become frustrated, full of hatred and malice, and try to take revenge in whatever manner they can. This explains why they react against Abrahamic religious symbols that HAVE NO MEANING TO Abrahamic (including non-Abrahamic ghosts).

What are you smoking nowadays? Weed?

Secretary: - You always taught us to be innovative, so I think this idea can be helpful.

But we are psychiatrists, Miss Roshini

Secretary: Sir, now, who is sophisticated and dull?

But will it work?

It is worth a try because it's mythical, and if we somehow make him believe she is gone... he will be fine...

Now you are also a part of this case...

We will meet his friends and family tomorrow, and yes, you will meet Nidhi also. Whom you are curious about.

"It is worth a try."

35
Cold eyes

Saturday, evening

Piyush, let's move... Dhruv is waiting.

Piyush: - tomorrow noon...

Now you should relax too, let us have a drink...

Hey Dhruv, have a drink. Let's enjoy...

.

.

.

Sunday, noon

Piyush: - "maa" [i got up and hugged aunty]

Sorry to call you for an urgent meeting, Uncle and Aunty.

Kamal: - not a problem, Mr. Viren; how is my son now?

He is showing improvement and a will to live...

Manju: - "Hey Prabhu, tera Shukria" [thank God]

Nidhi: - I want improvement in his health, not only willingness...

Roshni: - Sorry?

Don't mind Roshni. She is one boss lady, "Nidhi."

Miss Nidhi, I have requested to meet you all to share further plans. First, let me introduce you to Miss Roshni. She is my secretary, and she came up with an idea.

Nidhi: - Tell me the idea.

Piyush, what happened to her? Why is she so rude today? [said in a whispering tone]

Piyush: - she has been the same since Dhruv's discharge...
Okay...

Nidhi: - I am waiting to hear the idea...

Roshni, please do the honor...

Roshni: - as we know, his hallucination is related to mythology... so I feel there is no harm in taking a mythological route to make him believe she is gone...

Nidhi: - elaborate...

Roshni: - Does she do all the talking, sir? [in a whispering tone]

Don't get there, Roshni. You haven't seen her cold eyes yet...

Nidhi: - Mr. Viren, please tell Miss Roshni to elaborate...

Look, here are her cold eyes; please continue...

Roshni: - I want you to have a look...

The concept of exorcism found in Abrahamic cultures drastically differs from the Vedic Hindu perspective.

In Hinduism, we know that people "possessed" by hostile spirits are troubled by "hungry ghosts" who are stuck between dimensions and unable to enter the dynamic of reincarnation due to some severe karmic problem. Therefore, they are LESS POWERFUL than human beings and try to suck the energy of the human and use their body to perform actions they would not be able to do otherwise.

Hinduism offers the solution to APPEASE (tarpana) the poor, confused, and suffering soul by elevating its level of consciousness, presenting sacred water (usually from Ganga), sanctified food (pinda, etc.), and reciting the glorification of divine Personalities of Godhead from Puranas, etc. It is not an act of war but compassion comparable to the recently developed "secular" concept of "ghost whisperer."

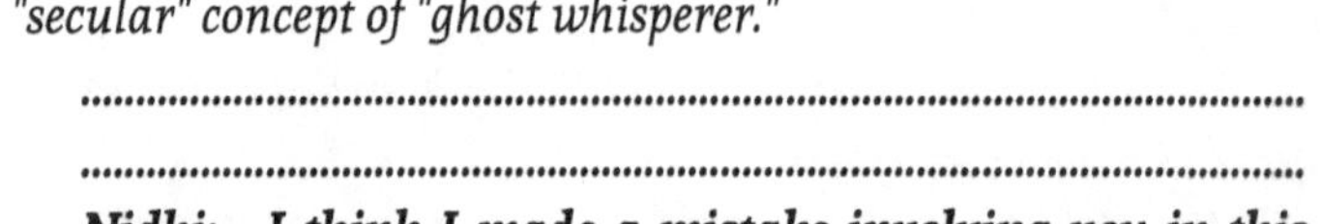

Nidhi: - I think I made a mistake involving you in this case... Mr. Viren...

Roshni: - How dare you?

No, no, no. Miss Roshni, calm down. We can't initiate any treatment for Dhruv without her permission. But Nidhi, please listen to her first...

Roshni: - Nidhi, think of a prospect we don't believe in. Please understand that he watched something on the podcast, started reading about it, became obsessed enough to meet a tantric, and got influenced by that tantric. And now he is hallucinating about that negative entity...

But he wants to be free, and if we make him believe that she is gone, he will start ignoring that hallucination... we will arrange this setup in a way that it will have no negative impact on his body...

Piyush: - Are you sure?

Nidhi: - And how do you know if it will work?

We can't just sit here and think it will not work; I think it is worth a try...

Piyush: - "Maa" what do you think?

Manju "Maa": - I want to meet my son, caress him, feed him food... Mr. Viren, you can do anything you feel like. I want my son...

Nidhi: - How will we do this?

Piyush looked at me, hearing Nidhi's approval [a sort of approval] ...

Nidhi, don't worry. I am emotionally connected to Dhruv and will not do anything that harms him.

Nidhi: - I don't want an assurance. I want a result...

Ouch, so cold... Miss Roshni, please lay down the plan...

Roshni: - we will contact our known "pandit." We will not tell him that we are thinking of this as a mental disorder... we will let him do as he likes but will make sure there is no physical harm involved...

{reason being we want Dhruv to feel and acknowledge that it is all authentic. If we don't do it, he will not ignore the hallucination}

Nidhi: - But where will we do it?

At Hanumangarh.

Piyush: - huh?

Yes, because we want to ensure he feels comfortable around his mother, and his fear of losing his mother and Nidhi disappears after the procedure.

Nidhi: - Mr. Viren, are you sure?

I looked at Piyush with disbelief because her tone {was low, and seems she was asking for help}

I am confident about it, Nidhi...

Roshni: - but sir, we need to talk to Dhruv first...

He is a younger brother to me now. He will not deny...

Nidhi: - If you are so sure, Roshni Mam... please do it as soon as possible... Aunty has been waiting for his son...

Roshni: - mam? Me?

"It is worth a try."

36

I want him to be Safe

—❦—

Monday

Dhruv, I want to meet you... I am coming... open the door.

Dhruv: - huh! Okay.

Why are you so tired?

Dhruv: - Her desire is getting uncontrollable.

OH... but I have found a way to free you from her...

Dhruv: - Viren, Are you serious? So, you mean I can meet my mother and go to college after that...

Yes.

Dhruv: Please tell me what I have to do.

Just trust me... and now take your medicine and sleep.

.

.

.

Roshni, Roshni...

Secretary: - yes, sir...

Leave everything and focus on Dhruv's case.

Secretary: - sir, I have already talked with a Pandit, but he wants to meet us first, and he wants to meet Dhruv also...

Then what are we waiting for? Let us move...

Secretary: - but sir, what about today's appointments...

Cancel them...

Roshni: - Namaskar Pandit ji, I called you in the morning...

Pandit ji: - where is Dhruv?

Huh!

Pandit Ji: - You Doctors think we don't care about people, but we do...

Pandit Ji, I want him safe... that's all I want.

Pandit ji: - where is he right now?

If you want, we can take you to him.

"I want him safe."

37
Will kill everybody

Roshni, are you alright?
Roshni: - yes, sir.
I know it is disturbing what we saw, but it's just a mental disorder.

.

.

.

Pandit ji: - where is he right now?
If you want, we can take you to him.
Dhruv, Dhruv... open the door...
Roshni, stay here...
Dhruv, open the door...
Dhruv: - huh! Viren, you again...
Crank...
Viren, umm... who is this?
Have a seat, Dhruv... Pandit Ji is with me.
Dhruv: - But why is he looking at me and smiling?
Before I could speak anything...
Pandit Ji: - I am not looking at you; I am looking at her... and want to talk to her.

And I thought this nuisance had started, but to make Dhruv Believe, I have to face this.

Pandit Ji: - what do you want from him?

Dhruv: - Huh!

"Tell him to leave."

Suddenly, Dhruv's body language changed. His face clenched, he started sweating, and his body stiffened. He glared over his shoulder, his eyes dilated, and asked for help.

Dhruv, what are you doing, Dhruv... why are you sweating? Why are you looking over your shoulder?

"Dhruv, tell him to leave."

Dhruv: - where are you?

Dhruv, with whom are you talking too?

Pandit ji: - she is whispering in his ears.

What the... Dhruv, please stop looking over your shoulder... Dhruv stop...

"Get out of here." [Dhruv spoke in a feminine voice, shrilling, harsh. Suddenly, room temperature decreased... my legs started trembling... Dhruv's body language got aggressive...]

What just happened? What happened to Dhruv? What happened to his voice...

"Get out of here." "He is mine." He is mine." I will take him away."

[this is not normal... something is going on here... I think there is a trigger point to all of this... I should have been careful...]

Dhruv, Calm down...

Shut Up... He is mine; I will take him away. Get out of here...

[shrill in his voice is pitching up higher now... he started to talk in a proper woman voice... from where did he learn this?]

Pandit Ji: - Viren ji, she won't do anything to him

Again, this nuisance...

Dhruv, calm down...

Pandit ji: - he is in control of "karnapisachani"

Hahahahaha... he is mine... go away... if you don't, I will take him with me right now...

{this is not good... we need to be quick now... he is losing it... the way his eyes are lifeless, if I don't do anything quickly, he might end up committing something fatal}

Pandit ji: - you will not harm him...

Hahahaha... really, umm...

{what the hell? Should I call for the sedative?}

Dhruv: - leave me... aaah...

Dhruv, please stop it. What are you doing? Leave your neck, Dhruv... {in the blinks of seconds, he is losing it. I need to get hold of him before he could do something wrong to his body}

Hahaha... "he is mine." Get out of here... get out...

Pandit ji: - leave his neck, and we will leave...

Dhruv: - save me, Viren... {why are my legs giving up on me? he requests me to help... but I can't even move an inch. What is this atmosphere? How well is he switching his voice?}

Hahaha... it was just a sample... if you try to take him away from me, I will kill everybody...

"I will kill everybody."

38
Chilling effect

—♡—

Roshni, if you want, you can take a day off...

Roshni: - Sir, we need to be quick. He is losing grip on himself... but what happened to his voice at that moment?

Bang...

Mam, mam, you can't just enter without permission...

Karan, stop... I know her, you can leave.

Nidhi: - what the hell was that? You promised me that he would not harm himself...

Nidhi, calm down...

Nidhi: Do hell with your words. What was that? Piyush called me and told me everything.

Calm down, have a seat first... shh... have a seat, and let me explain, please...

Nidhi: - Viren sir, please, I don't want any bogus words...

For the first time, I saw tears in her eyes... but I don't blame her. What I saw today left me shell-shocked...

Nidhi, this is the only way out. We need to be quick. His hallucination is taking over his senses... I was there. You heard what happened, but I saw it... I genuinely believe we need to make him believe that she is gone...

Roshni: - have some water, Nidhi... I have talked with Pandit Ji... he will provide us with the list of everything needed...

Roshni, please collect all the information regarding that "Vidhi" and be careful... I don't want any lapse in this case...

"What happened to his voice? It had a chilling effect on me."

39

But what if

Tuesday, morning

Roshni, 2 cups coffee

Roshni: - sir, you seemed tired.

Yes, I was reading about Schizophrenia and wanted to find out the reason for his voice change...

Roshni: - that was scary, sir

What is the progress?

Roshni: - I met Pandit Ji in the morning...

And?

Roshni: - he said he would perform a yajna, and he is ready to travel with us to Hanumangarh...

When?

Roshni: -Whenever we are ready...

And what is the procedure or ritual...

Roshni: - Pandit Ji said his assistant will take care of it...

Assistant?

Roshni: - but he said we must control Dhruv before taking him to Yajna...

Elaborate...

Roshni said he would give us the herb powder to help us control Dhruv...

What nonsense are we doing here, Roshni?
Roshni: - Sir, we have to bear it for Dhruv...
Call Nidhi and arrange a meeting with her and Piyush in the evening...
Roshni: - How's Dhruv, sir?
It was difficult to control him... everything I did in the last eighteen days is gone... and honestly, this might be our last try...
Roshni: - What do you mean by last try?
Piyush sent me a picture last night... Dhruv's back and chest are full of bruises... and it seems what we saw yesterday is not the first time that he has physically harmed himself...
Have a look...

.

last night
Piyush
new message

Have a look, Viren Sir. He felt uneasy while sleeping, and then I saw this. These bruises are all over his back and chest, and it seems like he is scratching not his body but his soul. Minor bruises, long bruises, some are fresh. Some are deeper than a knife bruise...

.

Roshni: Umm... sir, these bruises are from nails... and how can he do that to himself? On the chest, I can comprehend, but on the back, how?
When he grabbed his neck... for a second, I believed he would choke himself to death... his hallucination was consuming his senses, power, and ability to understand.
And you heard him. I will take him away... so he might try to harm himself, maybe fatally...
[Hahahahaha... he is mine... go away... if you don't, I will take him with me right now...]

Roshni: Sir, that voice still gives me shivers. We should abort this plan... it is risky now.... It seems like this is his trigger point.

We cannot abort the plan now.

Roshni: - but why, sir?

We have seen firsthand that his hallucination is so powerful that he is physically harming himself, so we need to make him believe that she is gone. And now he is not willing to wait anymore... if you have some other plan we can execute as quickly as this, then I am all ears...

Roshni: - but what if this went south?

In the best-case scenario, we might have to admit and keep him under observation...

Roshni: - did you say best?

Yes, the worst is we will lose him forever...

Roshni: - what about his family, Piyush, and Nidhi...

I don't know, but I am certain... it's our last try... and it is worth a try.

> *"But what if this went south?"*

40

We got this

Tuesday, Evening

Nidhi, why are you so quiet today? Is everything okay?

Nidhi: - why this meeting? [why is she so dull?]

We need to decide the day for the yajna...

Nidhi: So, are we following that path?

We need to... and Piyush, what is with this dull body language and quiet behavior... when I said it, I didn't think that a guy who has been rock solid from day one would break down.

He didn't just shed a tear. He cried like a kid...

"I can't see my brother like this anymore; he wants to leave that room; he wants to meet his parents; he wants to see Nidhi... he wants to live..." These were not the words; it was a cry of a grown-up man...

I tried to control my tears, but seeing tears in everyone's eyes... broke my resilience... I am a professional, but this case has become personal.

Dhruv's life is on the line, his parents' trust in God is on the line, a friend's resilience is on the line, and a girl's mental strength is on the line...

I got up from the seat, composed myself, and said Thursday is the "Day."

Inform Dhruv's Parents,

Roshni, get that herbal powder and tell Piyush what to do and when to do it.

Stay strong, guys...

"We got this."

....

Nidhi

Piyush, once you reach home, send me his picture...

"We got this"

....

Piyush

Please, God, Be kind to my brother...

"We got this"

....

Roshni

Viren sir is so engrossed with this case... I hope everything goes well...

"We got this"

....

Viren

Dhruv, please come out of it stronger than before... Nidhi and Piyush have faced enough... Now they need you... Please help yourself to help them...

"We got this"

Part 3

41

No time limit

Ayesha, mam, time limit exceeded, we need to wrap it up for today, said a crew member that brought me back to the present.

I am sorry, I didn't realize the time...

Ayesha: - No, this story will conclude today... no time limits. Viren, please continue...

Huh!

Ayesha: Yes, look at the live viewership. Everybody wants to know, and you already mentioned you need closure... so there is no time limit...

42

It's important

Thursday, 5:00 a.m.

Tring... Tring...

Huh! Roshni? I looked at the clock; it was 5 a.m... " **This early? I hope everything is fine with her.**"

Hello, Roshni... Is everything okay?

Sir, I will accompany you today...

What? It is not possible... Dhruv will be with me and... [before I could complete]

Roshni: - I know, sir, but I will be with Nidhi... she had booked a taxi...

Huh! How do you know that?

Roshni; - She is a boss lady, but still a kid... we are good friends now...

Okay, please reconfirm we need to reach Hanumangarh before noon, right?

Call Piyush and follow up about that powder... I don't want any lapse today, Roshni...

.

.

.

10:30 a.m.

Knock... knock...

Crank... *[As soon as the door opened, I got flagbasted]*

Piyush, what the hell, why is this room messed up so badly?

Piyush: - He might have lost weight but is still a gym rat. He was adamant about not drinking milk, but that was necessary for that herbal powder to work.

Piyush, you could have dialed my number...

Piyush: Leave it, sir. I am just happy that he will be alright after today.

Looking at his happiness made me nervous... such a big day [I whispered]

Piyush: - sir, shall we start our journey? It is 10:35

I was still in my thoughts... Huh! Yes, we should...

You were right, Piyush. He is one strong man. My back felt it when we picked him up... [I was trying to keep the surroundings relaxed because I was getting overwhelmed, and seeing Piyush excited made me nervous again]

He is assuming everything will be fine after today... but "what if"

No, no, no... don't you dare think negative, Viren [I scolded myself for having a negative thought]

Dhruv, my boy... don't you dare to give up on friends like Piyush and Nidhi...

Piyush: - Nidhi and Roshni have reached Dhruv's House. They will stay with Aunty until Pandit Ji completes the rituals...

Only after that will they come in front of Dhruv...

After the ritual, I will do a counseling session, and please make sure that no one will talk about it with him...

I want him to forget this part of his life altogether...

Piyush: - okay... sir, take a left from here...

11:50

What the hell is this setup? And why on earth is it that dark... Piyush careful

Kamal: - Dhruv, My son...

Manju: - I want to see my son.

Roshni: - aunty, not right now... just few more minutes...

Manju: - after so many days, he has entered his own house...

Nidhi: - Aunty, don't cry; you have waited for so many days; just a few minutes more...

Pandit ji, you said Yajna... Yajna setup seems different

[low on lights, and what is this boundary? And why are these windows open? The smell is different... and sacred thread all around this boundary...]

Pandit Ji: - Viren Ji, we know what we are doing? Your Patient will be fine after this.

Piyush, I have to take this nonsense for Dhruv, but make sure to show them the outside gate as soon as they finish their ritual...

Piyush: - sir, calm down...

Hmm...

.

.

.

12:00

Pandit Ji: - Kamal Ji, it is time to perform the Yajna... Viren ji, please bring him here...

But he is still Unconscious... in reply, Pandit Ji said, don't you worry, please bring him here and leave this boundary afterward, and everybody will stay back no matter what...

I did as Pandit Ji told me...

Piyush, what did he mean by "no matter what"? I don't care what he says, but if we see any physical harm to Dhruv...

we are stopping this.

Piyush: - huh! Okay... [he was startled by my attitude]

.

.

.

Piyush and I were busy in our conversation when Pandit Ji sprinkled some liquid stuff on Dhruv [later revealed as Gangajal]*, and Dhruv Got up and started yelling, which freaked us out...*

Dhruv Got up, and as soon as he saw Pandit ji, He started yelling at him...

"Why are you here? What did you do with him? Leave him alone; he is mine..."

Uncle and Piyush took a step back after hearing Dhruv's Voice [Voice I heard it before, so I was ready for it]

But as soon as Yajna started... he started screaming his lungs out... which caught me off-guard... [again that feeling of my legs trembling, the temperature decreased substantially]

he is mine... I will kill everybody...

Nidhi: - stop crying, Aunty.

Roshni: - Nidhi was trying hard to control Aunty, but she was equally afraid of whatever she heard. His Voice was shrill, and his yelling was turning into screams...

Piyush, stay focused. Don't let all of this affect you. You need to be mentally present here...

"You want to take him away from me?" "I will take him with me," came in a feminine voice... that sent a shiver down my spine...

Uncle fell as somebody pushed him... Piyush started tearing up... I took a step back.

Pandit ji: - leave him... "chali Jaa yahan se" [go away from here]

Aaah... save me Viren... Dhruv's Voice fills the room... *[he started changing his Voice so smoothly; please save him, God]*

.

.

.

Roshni: - aunty, believe...
Nidhi: - Was he screaming the same way when Pandit Ji met him for the first time?
Roshni: - it was less feminine...
Nidhi: - Roshni Di... are you sure it will help?
Roshni: - Nidhi, this is the last option...
Manju: - last option?
Roshni: - Viren sir told me that Dhruv's hallucination is overpowering him now...
Nidhi: - what do you mean?
Roshni: - If this doesn't work, we might have to admit him and keep him in a strict environment...
There were no words between them after that conversation...

.

.

Piyush... Piyush... take care of your uncle, and stop getting zoned out. It's important...

43

ॐ उग्रं वीरं महावष्णिं

ॐ उग्रं वीरं महावष्णिं ज्वलन्तं सर्वतोमुखम्। नृसिंहं भीषणं भद्रं मृत्यु मृत्युं नमाम्यहम्॥

Save me, Viren...

"He is mine. I will take him with me."

Dhruv cries filled the house, feminine yelling, Pandit ji hymns...

Feminine voice was tearing down our heads, Dhruv was coughing, and the war of resistance and trying to choke was one gruesome site...

I was getting restless. Piyush and Uncle were sitting like a lifeless body...

Suddenly, Dhruv fell... he was shivering... hymns were getting intense... feminine voices disappeared...

Pandit Ji got up from his position and tied a locket to Dhruv's hand. He then poured "Ganga Jal" on him...

Then, he put his hand on Dhruv's head and chanted a hymn before blessing him...

I looked at him, and when Pandit Ji smiled, it felt like I found a new life.

Piyush, Piyush... I yelled get up! We need to take him to his room...

As soon as It concluded, I started hearing knocks on the gate. "I want to see my son," Dhruv's mother's voice filled the room...

Piyush, let us take him to his room, then open that room but not let them in before counseling...

.

.

.

Manju: - Nidhi, I want to touch him...
Nidhi: - Just a few minutes...
Roshni: - ten minutes counseling it is...
                        Just ten more minutes, Aunty.

44

complex case

—♡—

Viren

Everyone is looking at me, waiting for the result... I am getting anxious now... wake up, Dhruv.

Dhruv: - huh! Cough... water, water...

I was sitting with my head down, but his voice made me excited and nervous simultaneously.

Dhruv, I quickly picked up the glass and offered him water...

Dhruv: - Huh! Viren, I am having a headache... Huh! Where am I?

*[as soon as he realizes he is in his room]***What the fuck... this is my room... I am at my house... viren what is going on? he started getting impatient**

Shh... listen to me... shh... where is she?

Dhruv: - she will come as soon as I call her...

Call whom? Nidhi?

Dhruv: - Viren, she will harm her. Please don't take her name...

Harm whom? Nidhi? Are you sure?

Dhruv: - What are you saying, Viren? I told you everything...

I remember everything, but you forgot, "I have found a way."

Dhruv: - Viren...

Shh... where is she? Look for her...

Dhruv: - umm... I want to see my mother... umm...

[after looking in all directions for two minutes, his facial expression changed. He was getting excited] **Viren, I hear no voices...**

I wanted to scream in joy, but I controlled...

Dhruv: - I want to see my mother... umm... viren... I don't hear her voice...

He wanted to jump in enjoyment but kept my grip tight...
Calm down, Dhruv...

Dhruv: - Viren, thank you so much......

Listen first... ask for sex *[I said in a whisper tone]* **and keep your voice low...**

Dhruv: - I want to have sex...

I looked toward the gate where everyone was standing, but fortunately, our voice didn't reach them...

Dhruv: - Viren [he screamed in joy] ... she is not here... she left me... he yelled excitedly.

As soon as he said it, I let his hand go... he jumped from bed... he started dancing... he was over the moon... he cried, laughed and hugged me then he ran out of the room... screaming in joy [Maa, Maa]

As soon as he saw his mother... he hugged her and then broke down... he kept apologizing and hugged his father...

Roshni and Nidhi embraced each other, and when Dhruv Hugged his father, Roshni and Nidhi embraced Dhruv's Mother...

Piyush was looking at everybody and was smiling *[what a gem of a person who is happy looking at people smiling]*

I went near him, hugged him, and intentionally shouted,

"Without you, it was impossible."

Dhruv heard it, and he came running toward Piyush and hugged him. That broke the ice, and I saw two friends letting their hearts out in the most beautiful way...

Manju: - Piyush, come here... You proved me right... I was right when I said my elder son is more responsible... you just saved your younger brother...

The emotion I saw in that room was unmatched...

Roshni: - sir, you seem so happy now...

This was my most complex case... and most emotional too...

Nidhi: - Thank You, Viren Sir...

Well, that's an incentive... boss lady...

Nidhi chuckled...

By the way, Nidhi, you have to take the initiative; he is looking at you but trying not to get caught...

Kamal: - Viren Ji, I won't say thank you because you are a part of the family now, and food is waiting for you...

Those words made me emotional... Dhruv gave me a big hug...

45

He is mine

Dhruv

What was I thinking when I made that grave mistake?

Look at this sight... Papa, maa, Piyush, Viren, Roshni Ji, and Nidhi together sitting and having lunch... spreading positivity around me...

But the biggest surprise is Nidhi... what a beautiful sight for a boy seeing his mother feeding with her hands to the girl he loves...

I apologized again... but everyone brushed that aside...

What a delicious meal it was...

Dhruv...

Hearing Nidhi's calling my name gave me some butterflies...

I turned around, but the guilt came running back... I lowered my head when I faced her...

Nidhi: Thank You for protecting me and keeping me safe throughout my college journey. You made some mistakes, but I am not angry. I am happy for you, and we will talk about it when we meet in college next time. So rest up and come back soon to college.

Huh! I am shell-shocked...

Nidhi: Look up, Dhruv. I am happy to see you back, and I will be waiting for you to rejoin the college.

I am unsure how to react, but she seems more beautiful by heart than I used to estimate.

.

.

10:30 PM
What a rollercoaster phase of my life...

But what a beautiful day it was... lots of talk, fun the whole day... but now I am tired... Maa is relieved now {but not before lots of love and scolding}

Piyush will get some rest, too... Nidhi will be feeling better now... and Viren must be happy...

I should sleep now...

.

.

Umm! Mosquitos inside the blanket...
"Haha haha..."
As soon as I heard that voice... my heart stopped... I opened my eyes and wanted to scream, but she didn't let me...
"You tried to betray me."
Umm... um... I wanted to speak, but my voice betrayed me.
"I will take you with me now."
Umm... don't harm me, is all that I could say...
"Shh... But before that, you need to be punished."
Umm... please [before I could say something]
"Shh... I will Kill your mother and Nidhi."
No, I screamed... please don't do this...
"Haha haha..."
Maa: - Dhruv... open the door
Maa... go a... [she didn't let me finish again, and asked me to open the door]
Clank...

I gathered my courage and said,

"Maa, run; she will kill you."

Splash... Splash...

.

.

.

"Dhruv"
Huh! When did I faint? Huh! Please leave me alone...
Umm! A fear gripped me when I saw blood on my face...
And then all the events before I fainted came back running to my head... I screamed, "Maa!"
I turned back, and then my soul left my body... I cried in pain, "screaming my lungs out."
Maa, papa... please open your eyes... maa...
It seemed like a blood bathtub. Blood all around me {blood of my parents} I cried, yelled, slapped me... I fucked up... "Maa, Papa."
"Haha." Now you have nobody here... you should come with me.
No, I screamed. Why did you do this?
No, you did this... you killed your parents. You did this for me.
No, you did it... I yelled at her
Shh... look at your hands; the knife is in your hands...
I threw away the knife; I wanted to touch my parents, but, in a way, she was right; I was the one who invoked "karnapisachani."
I am the Murderer...

"I killed my family."

"Dhruv, now you have to come with me."
I am ready...
"that's like a good boy," but I have a message for your friend

"HE IS MINE, I AM TAKING HIM WITH ME"

Can I write something too?
"Last message, Sure."

"I KILLED MY FAMILY"

46

Beep... Beep

Viren

Roshni, Good morning... Coffee for me.

Roshni: - well, our boss is happy today. Should we ask for a raise?

Done... 10% raise from this month on the name of Dhruv...

Roshni: - I should thank Dhruv then.

Good idea, I should call him...

He is not picking up.

Roshni: - Must be sleeping...

.

.

.

15 minutes later...

Tring... Tring...

Must Be Dhruv...

Huh! Piyush it is...

How are you, my boy?

Weep... weep... it is your fault... it is your fault...

Piyush, why are you crying? Piyush, first stop crying; tell me what happened.

Piyush: - Dhruv... {weeping, voice shivering}

Dhruv, what happened to Dhruv? And what is this distinct chatter around you...

{I got up from the chair and didn't realize when my hand touched the water jug and it fell to the ground}

"Whoop, whoop, whoop"

Ambulance siren, Piyush, why an ambulance siren... what's happening there? *{i was getting restless now}*

Piyush: - Dhruv, Uncle, Aunty is all dead *{weeping}*

What the fuck are you saying? Are you drunk? *{his words were echoing around me}*

Piyush: - turn on the TV; we lost them all... *{it is your fault, and I will never forgive you. It's your fault}*

Beep... beep...

Piyush... Piyush... what the hell...

Pick up the Damm phone... Piyush *{I screamed}*

Roshni... Roshni...

Roshni: - what happened, sir? Why are you yelling?

Turn the Damm TV on... quickly select a local news channel.

Roshni: - Huh! *{it is better to do whatever he says}*

Roshni, be quick... and Piyush, Pick up the Damm phone...

.

Breaking news
A horrific incident has lit up the Hanumangarh...
A tragic incident has turned this morning into a black day
for the city
A family of 3 {Husband, Wife, and Son} have been found
dead
Their names are "Mr. Kamal Sharma, Mrs. Manju Sharma,
and Dhruv}

.

Everything started to blur when I heard the name; nothing was audible...

The remote fell off Roshni's Hand. She was saying something, but it seemed my ears stopped working...
Roshni: - Sir, Sir...
Hmm... give me a glass of water...
After gulping a full glass of water... I regained some senses... I turned toward Roshni.
Roshni, we are leaving for Hanumangarh right now... but first, call Nidhi... and let me call Piyush again.

.

.

Roshni: - Hello, Nidhi...
I am Kritika, her cousin... Who is this?
[indistinct chatter] [crying voices]
Roshni: - I am Roshni, she knows me, can I talk to her?
Kritika: - I think you didn't get the news... She had an accident in the morning and is no longer with us...
Roshni: - what?
Roshni, what happened?
She waved at me to wait for a minute...
Roshni: - when did this happen?
Kritika: - in the morning, I need to go now...
Beep... beep...

.

.

Roshni: - Nidhi had an accident in the morning, and she is no longer with us...
What? [after giving me the news, Roshni falls on the seat]
What the hell is happening?
Roshni... Roshni... say something.
Beep... beep...
[WhatsApp: - 2 notification from Piyush]
Piyush has sent two images...

.

"HE IS MINE, I AM TAKING HIM WITH ME"
{it felt like the feminine voice I heard from Dhruv said this message in my ear}
"I KILLED MY FAMILY"
{Dhruv's Crying voice, which asked for my help, said this}

.

47

Viren: That was the most challenging phase of my life, and I decided to take a break from everything...

I used to hear Dhruv's Voice, which includes that feminine voice.

Ayesha- I don't know what to say, but I am feeling chills... my perspective toward that case just changed... but what happened to Piyush?

Viren: - He never contacted me again... nor picked up my call...

Can I get a glass of water?

Ayesha: - Yes, sure... Bring two glasses of water {One for Mr. Viren and One for me}

I don't know what to do, so I'll ask just one question. We'll leave the remaining questions for tomorrow.

Viren: - suits me as well...

"Was it a mental disorder, or was it a negative entity?"

I am sorry if I unintentionally hurt anyone's feelings. This is just a work of fiction, and it is not meant to hurt anyone's feelings.
Thank you for Your time and patience.

www.ingramcontent.com/pod-product-compliance
Lightning Source LLC
Chambersburg PA
CBHW051243130726
47988CB00001B/467